Clifford Harrison

In Hours of Leisure

Clifford Harrison

In Hours of Leisure

ISBN/EAN: 9783337848231

Printed in Europe, USA, Canada, Australia, Japan

Cover: Foto ©Andreas Hilbeck / pixelio.de

More available books at **www.hansebooks.com**

IN HOURS OF LEISURE

IN
HOURS OF LEISURE

BY

CLIFFORD HARRISON

LONDON

KEGAN PAUL, TRENCH & CO., 1 PATERNOSTER SQUARE

1887

CONTENTS.

CONTENTS.

Mother : to whom I owe the greater part
    Of all the little good I may have wrought,
To you, with humble hand and reverent heart,
    I dedicate this book, in filial thought.

Perhaps amongst its pages you may find
    Some echo caught from out your own sweet youth :
Reflected light from sunshine in your mind :
    Faint breathings of your own inspiring truth.

At Henley, often in my childhood's days,
    We walked, on summer eve, or radiant morn,
Through meadow, or through tangled woodland ways,
    Or where the poppies flushed the golden corn.

'Twas there you strove to give me eyes and ears,
    To see and hear, and heart to understand :
And I have striven hard these thirty years
    To learn the lessons pointed by your hand.

B

Over those lessons still my head I bow ;
For little known, alas ! as yet are they.
But you, who taught my feet to walk, will now
Forgive them when they stumble in the way.

And may I not, in giving you these lines,
Look back on him, to-day, who called you wife ;
Whose love still fills your lonely days, and shines
With faith whose roots involve the roots of life ?

And hope that still his pulses dimly move,
In all things following him I strive to do :
That so this book may doubly gain your love,
As sign that he still lives and speaks to you.

THE STATUE.

A VAST cathedral : here, a man of stone,
Above the long triforium, I stand.
I look to eastward, down the long dark nave,
To where the altar rises 'mid the apse—
Banners, and tapers, incense, flowers, and gold.
Beneath me stretch the aisles on either side.
And where the transept cuts across the nave,
The lantern-tower springs up beyond the roof.
My niche is carven, stool, and canopy,—
Acorns and oak-leaves, butterflies and birds,
And one small squirrel nibbling at a nut.
I always loved an oak the best of trees.
Certes 'tis very strange I should be here ;
Strange—and yet natural enough, in truth.
Most things seem natural when they come to pass.
I wonder how I look up here alone.

I take it no one knows me now I'm stone.
I scarcely know myself, or what I was.
'Tis evident I died some time ago ;
And now am turned to stone, and set aloft.
I never dreamed that such would be my end :
The ends we work for oft surprise ourselves.
I recollect 'twas often so in life.
But why this niche, and carven canopy ?
And why set up aloft, above the crowd ?
I do not think that I can be a saint :
I' the flesh I never was a saint, God knows !
I was as safe a sinner as the best.
But now I'm stone ; so I shall sin no more :
For sinning goes against the grain of stone.
Why I am here I think I'll never know.

'Tis rare to see the sunset and the dawn
Stealing athwart the walls, and o'er the roof.
'Tis rare to feel the sunshine warm my feet.
What time, like rainbows in the misty air,
The gorgeous colours from the painted glass
Swim all across the dark and solemn glooms.
Sometimes they make me glow from head to foot—
Ruby and amber, emerald and blue !

St. Matthew yonder, with the saffron robe,
In winter time, is first to take the dawn.
And when, from that clerestory window there,
The sunbeams strike that alabaster tomb,
I know that summer holds the outside world.
If I were man, with weak and dizzying brain,
I dare say I should sicken at this height.
I never liked to look from any height,
But now I like the gloom beneath my feet,
When dusk begins to work its mystery.
Then at the distant altar shine the lamps :
Then at the shrines the little tapers gleam :
And then, through windows where the glass is clear,
And piety has not yet made the light
Take up its parable for holy church,
I watch the gathering darkness find the stars.
Sometimes the wreaths of incense, rising high,
Will spread about the roof in silver haze,
And come between me and the world beneath,
Like summer clouds about a mountain gorge.
The air is always heavy with the scent,
Balsamic—full of comfortable warmth.
The only thing that really gives me pain
Is that strange shuddering that shakes the air

When the great organ mutters low and deep.
It shakes the very niche on which I stand :
It shakes my very inmost heart of stone :
And makes me think of what I used to feel,
Of what I used to do, when I was flesh :—
Of what those people feel who kneel in crowds
Far down beneath me—poor unsettled souls !
And for the moment I remember all—
Ambition—Love—and Grief—and all the rest.
And then it passes.   I am stone once more.

But yesterday I saw a man below,
Who beat his hands together on his breast,
And sank upon his knees, and hid his face.
And then I thought why I was like that once !
But now I'm stone, thank heaven ; and here, no doubt
I stand till Doomsday and the great white throne ;
Seeing the changing skies above my head,
And underneath my feet, the changing crowds.
I may outlive a dozen human lives.
The worst iconoclast would find it hard
To pull me from a perch as high as this.
No hands will touch me save the hand of Time.
I feel that I inherit centuries,—

Passionless, cold, immovable, and grand.
There are advantages in being stone.
You feel a level and profound content,
With just a wholesome touch of self-esteem.
Listen ! the Priest is chanting in the apse.
Now from the choir comes a sweet response.
That is the swinging of the thurible.
There goes the wreath of silvery smoke aloft.
Bells chime : and now with solemn tones
The organ takes the calm and reverent air.
Once I remember at a time like this,
I wept, and felt that I must cry aloud !
Oh me ! oh me ! I do remember all !
Ah ! how I loved her ! and she was so fair !
And shall I weep no more ?—Nay, but I will !
Now whilst the organ touches me with life—
Now whilst the music gives me memory !
Memory is Life ! help, Friends ! I live—I live !
I am not stone indeed—ah, help me down !
I move—I fall.—God help me !—so—I wake.

THE SPOILS OF MANDALAY.[1]

BENEATH the alien gray of Northern skies
They stand, the desecrated Sanctuaries.

The crowds pass by, unconscious : or, at best,
Give them an idle glance, or idler jest.

Some of those jewels, yonder, glittering,
In the regalia of the Burmese king,—

Girdle, tiara, sceptre, helmet, sword,
A veritable Nibelungen hoard !—

May have bedecked the monarch when his brow
Bent to these shrines, which no one bends to now :

[1] Lines written after a visit to the Indian and Colonial Exhibition, 24th September 1886,—to see the Sanctuaries from Mandalay.

For both are empty ; and 'neath each are writ
The few official words describing it—

"A Royal Sanctuary from Mandalay."
We see as we have eyes to see, they say !

The words mean little, or they mean so much
The mind shrinks back, half frightened from their touch.

Electric lamps will star the trees to-night ;
Fountains will pierce the dark with liquid light :

And the last waltz will echo clear and loud
Above the babble of the motley crowd.

But when the lamps die out, the crowds are gone,
The long unreasonable day is done,
And the slow tramp of watchman sounds alone

Along the silent rooms and corridors
That hold the riches of a hundred shores ;

The darkness must, one thinks, be all astir
With many an unshrined, spectral wanderer.

Strange gods, who seem to fix their cruel gaze
On blood-stained altars of forgotten days.

Idols from Lagos, and black Ashantee ;—
From coral islands of the tropic sea ;—

Uncouth and ghastly mockeries of man ;—
Old, immemorial gods of Yucatan ;—

The deities of all the Brahmin host,
From Himalay to Coromandel Coast ;—

Shapes of lost magic,—worshipped things, grotesque,
Painted on woods, in savage arabesque ;—

All these, methinks, must rise, when midnight comes,
To ghostly beatings of the fetish-drums.—

While high above them all, serene, might stand
The placid images from Buddha Land.

And what to them,—thus following the dream,—
The faith of this, their captor-land, must seem ?

Surely no sign of faith would they behold,
Save this—that England's god to-day is Gold.

Dreaming indeed ! For dead are one and all
Of those who look from shelf and pedestal.
No conjuration hath the power to call

Back into life the form of any god
On whom Time's hand hath written " Ichabod."

But though the glory be departed hence,
These empty shrines compel our reverence ;

Not only for the memories they give,
And for the pain of doom retributive
In things that sanctity and use outlive ;

But also for the bodeful thoughts they bring,—
Thoughts half of warning, half of questioning.

For eyes from this our western land are turned
To that great faith, whose unquenched light hath burned

From ages that most present faiths forerun,
Lighting the lands beyond the rising sun.

And Christians scan, with curious gaze afar,
The Christlike life and thought of Guatama.

Countless the years since Asia owned his sway,
And the first flowers upon his altars lay :

Countless the lips that still repeat each day,
" We refuge seek in Buddha," as they pray.

The countries, haply, whence the Wise Men came,
Worshipped at Buddha's shrines, and owned his name :

Ere yet Greece breathed beneath wise Solon's codes,
Or heard the music of Anacreon's odes :

Or ever on Jerusalem the weight
Of conquest fell from Babylon the Great ;

Shrines, like to these, in many an Indian grove,
May, unto struggling hearts grown weary of
Their burdens, and the bitterness of Love,

Have symbolised Nirvana, and have borne
The message of deep peace to lives forlorn.

And now, amidst the crowds who turn their eyes
On these deserted exiled Sanctuaries,

Are some to whom the sight may bring a sense
Of almost blasphemous irreverence,—
The world a loser with scant recompense,—

A deep regret for things torn from the place
They fitted well, and crowned with coarse disgrace.

And such might almost dream the day draws near
When these void shrines shall have a future here

Great as the past for which they now condone,
When their pale conquerors have learned to own
That he they shrined was worthy of a throne.

Long have we sent the missions far and wide,
To preach the gospel of the Crucified :

Is the day near when those to whom we preach,
The tenets of their older creeds will teach ?

Cities and empires, in the historic past,
Almost as great as ours, and nigh as vast

As that we own to-day by sea and land,
Before their fall,—when doom was close at hand—

Have turned, we know, with weak, half-hearted prayers
To gods dethroned and earlier faiths than theirs.

And 'midst the many signs, in many ways,
Marking the decadence of latter days,

Which seem at work amongst us now, there is
None that hath voice more sinister than this.

Therefore it is, that meaning nigh as great
As that these shrines had in their royalest state

They have to-day : they are a warning hand
From out the growing gloom of Buddha Land.

And so,—though crowds may pass them idly by,—
Though suns be dim for them, and dark their sky,—

These Sanctuaries—this one with fast-closed gate,
And open that, but both disconsolate ;—

With such surroundings as might suit a Fair,—
Our London's Champs Elysées,—still can bear

A strange significance which makes them rife
With power occult, and touches them with life :

With life not born beneath their native skies,
With power undreamt of by their votaries.

Our hands have borne them from their sunny East,
Robbed them of altar, worshipper, and priest ;
And yet in this thing they are royal, at least,—

That in the glittering of their glass and gold
A something lives which we may well behold

With national awe :—a message and a sign,
Scarcely less clear than that which once did shine,
Written in unseen letters, on each shrine,

When in the sun-blaze of the tropic day,
They flashed among the palms at Mandalay.

For—standing silent in this noisy air,
They say, to hearts that feel and ears that hear—Beware.

THE BELLS OF IS.

(WRITTEN FOR RECITATION WITH MUSIC.)

These lines are founded on an old Breton legend. M. Renan, in the Preface to his work, *Recollections of my Youth*, says :—" One of the most popular legends of Brittany is that relating to an imaginary town called Is, which is supposed to have been swallowed up by the sea at some unknown time. There are several places along the coast which are pointed out as the site of this imaginary city, and the fishermen have many strange tales to tell of it. According to them, the tips of the spires of the churches may be seen in the hollow of the waves when the sea is rough ; while during a calm the music of their bells ringing out the hymn appropriate to the day rises above the waters. I often fancy that I have at the bottom of my heart a city of Is, with its bells calling to prayer a recalcitrant congregation."

> THE bells of Is are ringing
> Far down my heart to-day :
> They call me to the memory
> Of scenes long passed away—

Of days almost forgotten—
    Of feelings long past by ;—
Sweet as the scent of flowers
    We loved in infancy.
The buried past is sending
    Its music up to my ears,
Through the seas that have flooded it over
    With the tangle and drift of years :—
Like bells from those buried cities
    The fisher folk tell us of,
Which they hear on summer evenings,
    As they float on the waves above.
The bells of Is are ringing
    With music so sweet and rare,
That the pathos of their message
    Seems more than I can bear.
And I almost find in my heart
    To cry to them, " Cease !   Let be !—
Let me hear the rush of the billow,
    The plash of the wind-rippled sea,
The noise of the wind in the cordage,
    The shriek, if you will, of the blast, —
But not that ghostly ringing
    From the bells of a buried Past !"

C

And yet their music is tender—
　　Those bells that rise through the wave !
And the ear still listens and listens ;
　　And the eyes pierce the watery grave,
In whose depths of transparent crystal
　　We re-make the Long Ago,
And see the past still standing
　　In a twilight world below.
Up, up through the waters welling
　　The memories rise amain :—
Regret that with joy is blended,
　　And joy that is fused with pain !

They are ringing to me the memory
　　Of a quaint, old-fashioned town :—
Red roofs beside a river
　　Where barges go up and down.—
Of days when wheat and poppies
　　And I were much of a height :
And the grass seemed a tropic jungle ;
　　And butterflies, blossoms in flight.
Of radiant summer evenings,
　　With voices of children afar ;
As lying awake, I would listen,

And watch for the evening star.
Of happy days on the river,
   'Mid lilies and meadow-sweet,
Where cattle knee-deep in the water,
   Stood screened from the noontide heat.
Of the lock, with its weirs and hatchways,
   Its woodwork and dripping moss ;
And the noise of the chain at the ferry,
   As the boat was punted across.
Of a dear, old-fashioned garden,—
   Roses, and sunflowers tall :
And the scent of the long box borders,
   And ripening fruit on the wall.

They are ringing to me the memory
   Of cloisters and chapel chimes :
And young romantic friendships
   In happy college times.
Of the tones of the distant organ
   Vibrating in the air ;
Till the very stones made answer,
   And hearing rose to prayer.—
Of hours with chosen comrades ;
   And unforgotten words,

That have grown to be the sweetest
   Amongst life's master-chords.—
And now I am hearing music
   On a silvery lagoon,
Where the marble walls of Venice
   Sleep in the light of the moon.
On, on in a gondola sliding,
   We float 'mid reflected stars ;
As, wafted over the water,
   Is borne the sound of guitars.—
A distant break of laughter :—
   The tolling of a bell :—
Dance music from a window :—
   A murmur of farewell.
A lonely mountain pasture ;
   Fir forests far below :
The moonlight on the glacier ;
   The sunset on the snow ;
The tinkle of the cow-bells,
   The plash of mountain rills ;
The avalanche's thunder
   Among the eternal hills.
The foam-flecked, gray Atlantic :—
   The blue, historic sea :—

All—each—up through the Present
　　Send voices unto me.

Oh, bells of Is! oh, bells of Is!
　　You ring of deeper things :—
Of thoughts that shrink from utterance,
　　Of high imaginings.—
Of love that lives for ever,
　　In spite of earth's "farewell":—
Of doubt too loud to silence :
　　Of faiths too dumb to tell.
Oh, bells of Is! oh, bells of Is!
　　Ring fainter, lower yet :
Be now your mystic message
　　In tenderest cadence set.
Speak of a face beloved ;
　　The memory of a kiss ;
A hand we daily long for ;
　　A voice we daily miss!

Oh, bells of Is! oh, bells of Is!
　　Deaf were the heart and ears
That never heard you ringing
　　Your psalm of vanished years.

The quaint old Breton legend
    Rings through our daily strife :
Its story is an image,
    A parable of life !—
When for a space we listen,
    As at some eventime,
And upward, through the Present,
    The bells of Memory chime.
Pause :—listen in the silence :
    Lest we their message miss !
Ring on—your heart-made music.
    Ring on ! sweet bells of Is !

THE SIGNALMAN.[1]

(WRITTEN FOR RECITATION.)

AT a level crossing far down the line,
Stood a signal-box with its points and sign.
White wooden gates railed off the road,
Save when carts went by with market load ;
Or some one drove to the little town
That stood at the bend of the far-off down ;
Or the labourers passed : or, night and morn,
The postman came with sound of horn.
The lamps burnt steadily all night,
Giving their silent speech of light.
Each shining green or crimson spark
Sent out some message through the dark.

[1] The leading fact of this story is a true one. I wrote it for
recitation in 1880. Since then the tale has become a popular one,
and many versions of it have been arranged for recitation.

And when the trains went by, by day,
The signals would change; and, far away,
The answering signs would fall or rise,
And the trains would whistle their shrill replies.
Hard by—in its strip of garden ground—
Stood the pointsman's cottage.　All around,
In marshy flats and meadows wide,
The country stretched on every side.
There pollards marked the river-brink;
And cattle, lowing, trooped to drink.
A line of aspens in the west;
A windmill; here and there, a nest
Of red-roofed, moated farms; great beds
Of water-reeds with plumy heads;
Straight roads, with dykes on either hand;
And miles on miles of pasture-land;
These gave the place its character.
A land where little seemed to stir!
Dreary, when skies were dull and gray;
But on a quiet, sunny day,
When the far distance melts away,
Having a beauty all its own:
A noble beauty that alone
The sea can rival or come near,

Of light and space and atmosphere.
Even the trains that onward tore,
With rattle and rumble and rush and roar,
Could not break up the peace serene
Of this sweet, pastoral, English scene.

Here lived the signalman.   His post
Demanded care and trust, almost
As great as any man alive
Could well be called upon to give.
The man is worth a passing gaze :
A hero in his humble ways.
His face is bronzed with tropic clime.
In India he had served his time
In some line-regiment.   Now had come
To this spot :—pleased to find a home
Near to the place where, years before,
He met the girl to whom he swore
His faith : who, to the Indian shore
Followed her soldier-husband : there
To die—and leave, as token fair
Of love, one child—a girl.   This child
Tamed in him all that once was wild.
She grew for him the life of life ;

Centering his love for child and wife.
She now was barely four years old :
Rosy cheeks, and hair of gold,
Eyes that held the sky's blue rays,
Dimpled limbs, and winsome ways,
Made her such a thing of light,
You seemed the better for the sight.
And everything he did or sought
Was hers, and looked to her, in thought.

See him now, one summer's evening,
   In the garden, hard at toil ;
Plucking weeds from 'mongst the blossoms,
   Breaking up the sun-dried soil.
Hear him whistle, happy-hearted :
   Now, a moment, see him stand,
Whilst the child's soft little fingers
   Clasp his strong and tawny hand.
Sweet ! how sweet it is ! and peaceful !
   From the golden meadow land
Comes the laugh of schoolboys, bathing ;
   Broad, the sun hangs in the west ;
Thrushes sing on leafy copses ;
   Rooks fly, cawing, home to nest.

With a childish laugh of gladness,
    Turns the little maid away ;
Seeing some new flower to gather,
    Or some fresh device for play.
Then he stoops, and goes on working,
    Thinking of the days gone by :
And his thoughts go fleeting eastward,
    And he sees the Indian sky.
Overhead the great bananas
    Stretch their palm-fronds, broad and flat :—
Now he hears the drum and bugle :—
    Now he—— listen ! what was that ?
In the far, extremest distance,
    Sound like thunder, faint and low ;
And he lifts his head and listens ;
    Then he puts down spade and hoe.
The train is due—the down express.
Do you not hear it ?—listen :—Yes.
Like to the noise of muffled drums,
Through the quiet air a faint pulse comes.
There ! do you hear it ?—there again !
At yonder junction another train
Must wait for this to pass.   The sign
That tells that other train the line

Is blocked to it, or stands at "clear."
Is, by this pointsman, worked from here.
So the fate of the train that onward comes,
   And of that which at the junction stands,
Depends on the signalman turning the points :—
   Their hundred lives are in his hands.
The gate that leads to the line is ajar—
   Strange ! for 'tis always his thought and care
To keep it closed—so he makes it fast,
   And goes to the foot of the wooden stair.
Hark ! the signal-bell's "ting, ting,"
And the wires jerk and swing :—
And nearer, nearer, nearer,
And clearer, clearer, clearer,
Comes the rattle, and rumble, and roar, and shriek :
And he goes to the points—when lo ! his cheek
Is blanched as with sudden frost of death,
And his eyeballs start, and he gasps for breath :—
He cannot move—he cannot speak—
He tries—but tries in vain—to shriek !
All strength from limb and spirit fails.
For he sees—his child—between the rails.
Sleeping, she lies there, bright and fair,—
Low on the ground shines her golden hair :—

In his soul the conflicting storm grows wild,
    As the questions go up, with maddening cry :—
Shall he do his duty ? or save his child ?
    Which *is* his duty ? great heaven, reply !
And nearer, nearer, nearer, nearer,
Clearer, clearer, clearer, clearer,
With rattle and rumble and roar and scream,
The train comes on like a terrible dream.
It is rushing onward to certain doom.
It is almost here.   He sees it loom
Through the mist in his eyes.   In his hands is its fate.
In another moment 'twill be too late.

The soldier-instinct of former life
Comes back in that moment of awful strife.
Like a bugle-call Duty speaks, clear and plain :
    He leaps to the signal : he seizes the rod :
He turns the points : he saves the train :
    And trusts his child to God.

And not in vain was that heaven-born trust.
    For the train rushed by with fiery breath ;
It faded away with its cloud of dust ;
    And then came a silence as of death.

To open his eyes he did not dare,
  As, with hand on the rod, and teeth hard set,
He stood like a statue, motionless, there,
  His pallid brow with anguish wet.
When a child's laugh rang out, sweet and clear :
And the one word, " Father !" fell on his ear :
And he turned and looked : and there, behold,
Shone the rosy face, and the tresses of gold !
The train had passed over the child, as it fled,
Nor injured a hair of its little head.
And she ran to him, clapping her tiny palms,
  And, wondering, asked what it was, and smiled :
And the strong man caught her up in his arms,
  And wept like a little child.

THY KINGDOM COME![1]

Thy Kingdom come. Sore need I have, Thou knowest,
  That it should come, and quickly, unto me;
Before I sink still nearer to the lowest,
  And lose the far-off light that yet I see.

My Kingdom,––Lord, its glory is departed;
  Its palaces are low; its skies are gray:
And here I sit, 'mid ruins, listless-hearted.
  " Thy Kingdom come," is all that I can say.

Thy Kingdom, in its splendour and its beauty;
  Let now its reign of freedom come to me.
" Nay: rather, up! and get thee to thy duty:
  Seek for it there, and it shall come to thee."

[1] Published in *Good Words*.

TO SOME FIR-TREES.

Gazing across the valley, I see,
  O'er the spires and roofs of the town,
A mile away, or more it may be,
  The crest of a noble down.

Often the smoke from this factory place
  Curtains it out from view:
And often its form I can barely trace
  In mysterious lines of blue.

But when a sunset breaks through the cloud,
  And blazons the sky with gold;
And the work is done, and the smoky shroud
  Down the distant valley is rolled:

I, sitting out here on the window-sill,
    See, pencilled against the light,
A tuft of fir-trees, afar, on the hill,—
    The crown to its topmost height.

They tell me that, though from the chimneys afar,
    They are blighted by poisoned wind :
But to me they seem, and to me they are,
    The kindliest of their kind.

For they seem to possess a magical power
    To whisper my spirit away
From the noise of the street, the fret of the hour,
    The weariness of the day.

I forget the clangour of hammer and plate,
    The clash of irons and steels ;
I forget the air with its smoky weight,
    And the clatter and whirr of the wheels ;—

And I see calm rivers embosomed in wood ;
    And lakes that are clear as glass ;
And gardens in June, when the air is good
    With the scent of new-mown grass.

D

Anon under windclipt oaks I lie,
  On the slope of a hill : and below,
The seagull utters its lonely cry,
  And the waves are broken in snow.

The cuckoo is calling from woods afar ;
  I can hear the weir at the mill :
And the church-bell chimes, as the evening star
  Shines over the edge of the hill. ,

Such scenes I see as I gaze at those trees :
  They have made many moments bright :
And have linked themselves unto memories
  That carry a lifelong light.

Thanks, thanks, O fir-trees on the hill
  That stands above the town !
Ere I leave this city of forge and mill
  I shall climb that distant down ;

And when I reach you I'll bend the knee,
  And greet you with loving signs :
And wish you a worthier eulogy
  Than is chanted to you in these lines.

IN THE LAUTERBRUNNEN VALLEY.

THE sunlight climbed aloft an hour ago.
We watched it creeping up the mountain wall—
A gray shade rising, whilst the glow above
Deepened until it seemed to burn the rock.
Now all is growing dusky : and a sense
Of something supernatural holds the place.
The river, hoarse with telling secrets dark
Of its high glacier-prison far away,
Answers the softer and continuous voice
Of waters filmed and falling in mid air.
But these are sounds that make a solitude :
And other sound is none.   The stir and life
That buzzes yonder, two miles off or more,
Has long been lost.   These mountain vales and heights
Are strong and big enough to hold their own
'Gainst all the noisy crowd that does its best

To spoil and mar the beauty that it seeks.
We walk a little way from off the road,
Press farther than the cluster of hotels,
And nature meets us with as full a face
As we can bear to look upon : sometimes
So full we have to drop our eyes in awe.
What are the subtle secrets and the hopes
That lay their spell upon a scene like this ?
An unknown and unanswered question lies
Across it.   Let it be : and look and look,—
And live in looking :—'tis enough.   To look
A lifetime were to leave a world unseen.

The dusk has deepened.   Here and there 'twould seem
That night already has begun its reign.
The narrow strip of valley would be dark
But for the light reflected from a cloud
That holds the sunset which we cannot see.
Between the fields the road winds on and on,
Through giant gateways of the towering rock,
To where the glacier closes up the vale
And thunders downward on the Schmadribach.
The strip of sky looks strangely far away ;
And gazing up the eastern precipice

Between a chasm in the rock, behold !—
Thousands of feet above us in the air,
The Eiger all transfigured into flame,—
Ablaze with sunset,—golden 'gainst the blue,—
A fairy world of glory and of death !

It is a scene of wonder and romance.
I have no power to put it into words;
But I have heard it all, and felt "'tis there !"
In some of Wagner's music.   Yes : *it* said
Something akin to this.   And you, my friend,
You hear, and feel it too, and understand.
We look, and look, and see it plainly writ :
We listen, and we hear it clearly.—What ?
Ah ! for the Name !   I wrestle, and am lame.
But we are not alone : and other eyes,
And other ears, have seen and heard as well :
Ay, see and hear with fuller sense than ours.
We stretch our hands to them : they understand.

CARCASSONNE.

(WRITTEN FOR RECITATION.)

Adapted from a song by Gustave Nadaud.

THE lovely valley of the Aube leads down
To Carcassonne, an ancient Roman town.
Far off, above the nearer hills, one sees
The ridges of the Eastern Pyrenees.
Some half way up the valley stands Limoux.
The only thing that once would hurry through
The village was the stream that gave its name
Unto the vale.   The summers went and came ;
The seasons changed : but other change was none.
It lived its own life.   Till ten years agone
The busy world stopped short at Carcassonne.

And in this quiet nook of southern France,
With days that knew small touch of variance,

A peasant lived who never once had been
More than a few short miles away, nor seen
A larger place than this Limoux.   To him
The outside world was mythical and dim.
Toulouse—and Paris—and Bordeaux—and Rome,—
Ah, yes : they all were there :—but this was home.
One place he longed to see, and only one :—
He'd meant to go, and yet had never gone :—
It was the city yonder—Carcassonne.

He said, " I'm growing old.   Nigh seventy year
I've lived my life, and worked the months round, here.
And yet—I doubt not wisely—God has willed
My fondest wish should never be fulfilled :—
A wish that I have fostered since a lad,
The one desire that I have always had.
But now I know—we learn it often thus
In disappointments that are sore to us,—
There's perfect happiness on earth for none.
I shall not have my wish fulfilled for one :
No, I shall never go to Carcassonne.

" One sees the town upon a clear, fine day
Beyond the mountains yonder, far away.

To reach it you must go across the plain :
'Tis five leagues there, and five leagues back again.
They say the road's a good one ; and I've known
Folks who have gone there, all the way, alone.
Ah ! if the vintage were but good this year !—
The grapes will not turn yellow yet, I fear—
But if the sun had only brightly shone
Prosp'rous the year had been for every one ;
And so I might have gone to Carcassonne.

"They tell me that each day, week in, week out,
A week of Sundays, every day, no doubt,
One sees crowds always going up and down,
Hither and thither all about the town.
And on the promenades and terraces,
Smart dresses, music, everything you please !
Nay : you may even see, at one time, there
A Bishop, and two Generals ! you stare !—
'Tis true.   A castle too—a mighty one !
Huge as the palaces of Babylon !
Think of it, sir !—and all in Carcassonne !

"The Curate he was right, that I confess :
He spoke the very truth and nothing less.—

'We look too high, we want too much,' said he—
A sermon to remember,—'for, you see
How often thus by our desires we fall :
Ambition, O my friends ! destroys us all.'
Quite true.   But, all the same, if we should get
A few nice days of pleasant weather yet,—
Say two or three,—before October's gone,—
Mon Dieu ! I then would say Thy will be done !—
I still might get as far as Carcassonne.

"Ah, God forgive me, if my prayer be wrong !
One always wants too much, no doubt, as long
As life remains.   Ambition ?—yes—it's true.
But still I'm sure it must have fall'n to you
To see some men get what they want, yet be
No whit the worse :—well now, that puzzles me.
My godchild—she is married now—has seen
Perpignan—yes, sir : and my wife has been,
With our son François—not to go alone,—
As far (you'll scarce believe it !) as Narbonne !
But I—I've never been to Carcassonne.

"Is it a foolish and a sinful thing,
This wish ?   Peace and contentment age doth bring

In much—I have my work when I am strong ;
I get to church ; and, when the days are long,
I do my bit of gardening.　'Twould be wrong
To say that there is much that I regret.
No : still I'm bound to say there lingers yet
That one wish of my boyhood—that alone.
I'm sorry.　But it's true I have that one.
Yes, I should like before my life is done—
I should !—I should !—to go to Carcassonne."

"Cheer up, old friend, for go you shall !" I cried.
"Ay, and we'll go together, side by side.
We'll go to-morrow if the day is fine."
And in a brimming glass of good white wine
We pledge good luck to the auspicious day.
We started.　All the world was bright and gay.
The village all came forth to see us start.
We sat beneath the awning in the cart.
And as we passed along a sweet smile shone
Upon his face, as he, to every one
We met, cried out, "I go to Carcassonne !"

Down through the valley, and across the plain ;
Over the Aube, made hoarse with autumn rain ;

Past dusty thickets where the crickets sing :
And vintage walls where fruit was ripening ;
Through busy little towns and villages,
Where folks were sitting underneath the trees ;
We drove.   The diligence went past anon.
A cart with oxen yoked came slowly on.
And then, just where the cross roads meet in one,
We saw the sign-post.   Half the way was done.
I pointed out the words—" To Carcassonne."

But ah ! may heaven forgive us all, say I,
For, as we halted in some shade near by,
I turned, I say, to point the sign-post out.
He had been silent for some time.   A doubt
Struck on me.   " Are you tired, old friend ?" I said.
He answered not.   I touched him.—He was dead.
Bells on the harness jingled.   Far away,
The great plains sleeping in the sunshine lay.
The road, a long white line, before us shone.
A clock struck noontide.   Half the way was done.
But he—he never went to Carcassonne.

Limoux is changed.   Since then its quiet ways
Have heard the roar and scream that nowadays

Alters for good or ill all places such
As this.   And Carcassonne—changed too?   In much,
No doubt: but not that Carcassonne he sought.
Changing for all, it still is changed in nought:
For it is built upon enchanted ground.
Ah! who has seen it? was it ever found?
Think not this peasant only, he alone,
Dreamt of this place: 'tis nigh to every one.
For all the world there is a Carcassonne.

A PROTESTATION.

My life has laughed to scorn my lip's white creed;
    To Faith I oft have bent a trait'rous knee;
I have been liar both in word and deed :—
      But have been true to thee.

My heart is like the trodden sandy beach
    That every tide will wash and smooth anew :—
But I have graved, beyond the billows' reach,
      " Fidelis " unto you.

I crowned myself with weeds and poison-blooms;
    Blistered life's brows with hemlocks of the dead :
Bedecked my shrines with flowers fed from tombs :—
      But lilies for your head.

I have not done one thing 'twere well to do ;
    I have been false to all things that are true :—
But—thro' the darkness one far glimpse of blue !—
      I have—God knows—loved you.

TO THE DEPARTING SUMMER.

THE light is going from us day by day,
    And darkness spreads his kingdom in the night :
To other lands the summer fleets away,
    Breaks from our grasp, and passes from our sight.

Something has gone more precious than the rose—
    A spirit, leaf or blossom far above :—
Something no words can ever quite disclose—
    Voiceless as joy, yet sensible as love.

The air with growth no longer now is rife :—
    The land holds not those rich exuberant powers,
That almost satiate the heart with life,
    And make the very grass burst forth in flowers.

Now could I seek, as swallows seek, a shore
    Southward and sunward, far from Northern frost,
Where I might find blue sky and flowers once more,
    And overtake the summer we have lost.

Yet I do Summer-time so well adore,
    And treasure up so tenderly her smile,
That if her absence makes me love her more,
    I willingly will part with her awhile ;

Nor, with irreverent and intemperate feet
    Pursue her wildly : but, content, await,
Till she return, grown doubly dear and sweet,
    Love to reward and Joy to recreate.

TO A PEAL OF BELLS.

Oh, sovereign bells, your music troubles me ;
　　It sounds so joyous, and a speech so clear!
And yet the joy is veiled in mystery :
　　The speech, an unknown one, to any ear.

I cannot settle to my work.　A flush
　　Fevers my hand and heart.　All things around
Seem poor and trivial in the clang and rush
　　Of your imperious and compelling sound.

Oh the sweet clamour! how it fills my ears,
　　And probes me with unreasonable regret,—
With hopes of what I know not—shadowy fears,—
　　With days gone by—and summers that have set.

With hours of sorrow and of festival—
   Almost with thoughts of having lived before—
With painful efforts vainly to recall
   Something forgot, or gone to come no more!

I wish that you would cease, O tyrant bells!
   You come between me and my life to-day.
O'erpowered by your strong but nameless spells,
   I wait until your reign has passed away.

E

THE FRIENDS.

It was a day so wonderful to me
That, looking back across the level plain
Of weeks that knew small change of scene and thought,
It rises like a richly-wooded hill
Lit with the glow of " Memory's sunset light."
I thought that it would be a tedious day :
For they, you know, were going out to spend
The day in open air, with picnic feast.
" And you, too," Arthur said, " are going out
To see great sights, and breathe a summer air,
In this new poem by the Laureate."
And laughingly he brought the book to me.
I took the book, but could not answer him
With badinage : for I was vexed or sad.
Patience is difficult when days are bright :

'Tis hard to be, amidst the general song,
A dumb, dead note that answers not to touch.
And so, with silent lips, and face that wore
A smile with lamentable want of grace,
I listened to their "*Au revoirs.*" And then
I heard their happy voices as they passed
Adown the lawn, and sloping shrubberies,
To where the boat was waiting them below.
Then came the sound of mooring chains unloosed :
And then anon the rhythmic pulse of oars :
And then I fear some tears of fretfulness
Made dim my eyes with vain but sharp regret.
For then the narrowing circle of my life,
Had but begun to close and shut me in,
And all the weight of loss was new and strong.
But none was happier than was I that day.
And thus it came about. My fretful heart,
As is its custom from my boyhood's years,
Full soon began to soothe itself with song.
Song, quotha?—doggrel of the tritest rhymes :
And somewhat morbid too, and weak of heart :—
A poor thing, verily: but yet its own.—
And therefore sweet and full of calming strength.
The uncut book that Arthur gave to me

Was held irreverently to make a desk.
I fear the sacred flame that lay within
Gave out no spark of its Promethean heat
To touch my pen with any answering fire.
I cannot now recall a single verse.
Indeed I soon put pen and book aside
Before a score of lines were pressed to shape :
Forgetting them, and all my fretfulness,
In calm renewal of a healthier mind.
Shall I not therefore love my humble Muse?
For such the work she wrought in me that day :
And such the work she oftentimes hath wrought.
Many the weary hour that she has cheered :
Many the pain her songs have lulled to sleep,
Or brought me strength to bear : and many, too,
The Beauty she has nursed, and brought to sight,
The Evil she has robbed of Victory.

Between the woods and water meadowland
The sloping fields were golden-gray with wheat :
And one was scarlet with the poppy blooms.
The hills above the woods rose into downs,
With here and there a gleam of silvery chalk.
A clump of firs, a zigzag clambering path.

Far down the valley, hazy with the heat,
A line of poplars rose beyond the bridge
That winds, with quaint uneven arch and curve,
Across the broad and shallow river-bed.
Even the farthest hills were pencilled clear :
But faint in depths of sunlit atmosphere.
The air blew on my face, fulfilled with scent ;
Remembrances of rose and mignonette,
With messages from clover fields abloom.
In those sweet wafts of spice I seemed to taste
The breath of zones that lie beneath the sun,
And strange impressions I had never felt
Of scenes and countries I had never seen,
Rose on me like forgotten memories.
Faint bleatings came from off the meadowlands.
Jetty, the cow, went wading through the pool :
Whilst underneath the ample spreading elms
The sheep were gathered, screened from noontide heat.
A flying, twittering band of swallows came,
Skimmed past the window toward the o'erhanging eaves,
And thereon held a moment's parliament.
The cuckoo knew its latest day had come,
And told its name once more to all the hills.
The blackcap whistled loud in neighbouring copse,

And drowsy answers from the dovecot near,
Soothed all the air with cooing lullabies.

An unseen world was my real world that day;—
The spirit-world that we call Memory,—
As real a world as Love, or Faith, or Hope!
I journeyed far in thought : and heard and saw :
And lived in everything I saw and heard :—
And came home richer, ay, and happier too!
Home ?   To myself, my chair, this room, the hour !
These were the home to which myself came back—
From journeying, whither ?   It seems hard to tell.
Say—in the world that lies within us all.
Within us, and around us, everywhere.
Life is so busy nowadays, things seen
Are so imperious in their thousand claims,
We seldom take these journeys.   Well, perhaps,
So best.   A question.   Some might say 'twere time
Wasted, to take these unseen journeyings.'
If so, I always "wasted time," I fear ;
And even think that "wasted time" well spent.
The gain to me was often definite ;
Intangible, and hard to put in words ;
Only to be translated into life

And living :—but, when once translated thus,
Discernible and sensible to all.
Yes : just those "wasted" times are now to me
The only life I have : and from their work
My present life is made.   For what the world
Calls life is closed to me.   This room were it
Save for that unseen world of which I speak.
But now the room seems wide as any world,
And I live in it, happy and content.
Nay : I am bold to fancy, on that day,
I, lying dreaming on my sofa here,
Did more, and gained more positive reward,
Than some that found a task for every hour,
Or on whose books the day filled many a line.
There's self-conceit !   At least 'tis evident
The good I brought back from my unseen world
That I belaud so lustily, possessed
A saving grace of human vanity.

The sun was shining.   Out I went in thought,
And wandered through a hundred pleasant scenes.
I half-believe that Fairies (for, you know,
I always did my best to keep their haunts
Undesecrated) came to me that day,

And conjured up these well-beloved scenes.

My words would do them wrong, and blurr their truth.

Go out into the garden, down the lane,

Across the hill, by river, wood, and field.

The scenes will not be clearer to your eyes

Than were their shadows unto me that day.

One only will I tell you of :—the names

Alone will paint the scene to you—

Lac Leman, and the slopes above En Caux !

Ah! you remember it as well as I.

Some days are festas in our lives—bright days,

Mostly unheralded :—and that was one.

You know the scene so well ! better than I :

I often see it in remembrance.

And once whilst lying on that mountain side,

In thought, I put remembrance into words :—

> Oh the lovely light that lay
> On the mountains far away,
> That delicious summer day !
>
> When we rested from the heat
> In the pinewood, cool and sweet ;
> Whilst the world lay at our feet.

Butterflies, with colours pied
On their gorgeous wings spread wide,
Came sailing down the mountain side.

In a wood-trough, quaint and old,
Water, crystal-clear and cold,
Dripped through mosses green and gold.

Then we left the arching trees,
Coming out on terraces
Starred with lilac crocuses.

Still we climbed on, up to where,
From the open hillside bare,
Came the wine-like mountain air.

Silent ! nothing could be heard ;
Not the song of any bird ;
Not the sound of aught that stirred :

Save the murmur, soft and sweet,
Born of life and noontide heat
'Mong the grasses at our feet ;

And the cow-bells, far away,
Tinkling from the fields that lay
On the lower slopes of Naye.

Silence, ample and intense,
Filled the heart and every sense
With a natural reverence.

There, upon the flowery grass,
Down we lay : and never was
Hour that did so quickly pass.

High above the world we seemed ;
Over us the white clouds dreamed :
Far below the blue lake gleamed.

Mile on mile, it stretched away
From the Jura's sunlit gray,
To the woods of Bouverêt.

Glittering like a silver throne,
High the Dent du Midi shone
O'er the Valley of the Rhone.

Very faint and far below,
Rose the poplars, row on row
Where the water-lilies grow.

Tiny wings upon the lake,
Sails of barques the light would take :
Long lines curving in their wake.

Every moment wonder grew :
Every moment beauties new
Seemed to rise upon our view.

And our hearts as we lay there
Were as free from stain of care
As the stainless summer air.

And we vowed nor pain nor change
Ever should our hearts estrange,
Whereso'er our paths might range.

Earth such youth and freshness wore,
Seemed as though the vow we swore
Never had been vowed before :

Seemed as though a vow so sweet,
Made in time and place so meet,
Could not ever know defeat.

But the bright hours would not stay :
That sweet happy summer day
Passed with all good things away.

Yet it left a memory
Which Time cannot teach to fly,
Which will never pass us by.

And a lovelier spirit-light
Than mere sunshine, howe'er bright,
Makes it holy in our sight.

Yes : makes it holy, for such hours are blest.
The consecration of a perfect joy
Doth rest upon them, setting them apart.
Many and bright the scenes I saw that day :
And found in all the joy of very life.—
Moorland and meadow ; lane and sandy beach ;
The perfumed forests of the Haute Savoie ;
The chalêt where we spent those happy weeks

Beneath the Jüngfrau's crown of virgin snow ;
Sweet Maggiore sleeping in the light :
Dalhousie's woods ; and Clifton's hawthorn groves ;
An orchard on the hillside, looking down,
Through apple-boughs thickset with golden fruit,
At silvery surf that ripples on the beach
A hundred feet below us—and the Bay
Curving, with richly-wooded cliffs and coombes,
Away to red-rocked Portledge, and the Bar,
And Exmoor melting in the summer clouds.
I will not weary you by telling more
Of what I saw or where I went that day,
In thought : or with how real an eye
I seemed to see the scenes of memory.
So passed the morning light to afternoon.
Then whilst I read the perfect verse that tells
Of that poor "Scholar Gypsy"—poem beloved !—
Where Oxford, like a spiritual Thebes,
Builds itself up upon a poet's song,—
I heard a footstep more than song to me,—
A footstep that I little dreamed to hear,
Thinking the foot was many miles away—
And you came in—welcome as Health itself !
Then, with surprise and pleasure, how you came,

And why, where you had been, and whom had seen,
With frequent question met by swift reply;
And all the joy of friends who meet again
After long absence marked by many a change,
To find their love unchanged amid it all,
The hour of sunset came ere we had ceased
To feel the wonder of the clasping hand.

My life has moved in very narrow grooves.
As I review it, lying passive here,
It seems, by turns, pathetic, or to touch
On something almost humorous—'tis so small !
There's many a boy who has not left his teens
Is older far than I, and takes his place—
And is allowed it—in the world : whilst I,
At thirty, seem a sort of grown-up child,
Who has his toys, and lives a little life
That does not fit the fashion of the world.
Oh ! I assure you I am much amused
To look, as an observer, at myself.
And I can add up all that I am worth,
Subtract, divide, and give you the result
With an exactness that is excellent.
I think too much about myself ?   No doubt.

In that at least I fit the world to-day.
We modern folk are students of ourselves.
We like to know our mind's anatomy :
Or better still, anatomise our friends !
Some that I know would almost like to ascribe
A motive to the sun for shining so :
But it is true, I'm quite ashamed to own
How much I find I interest myself !
Well, those I love seem vital parts of Me,
And so the interest is not wholly Self.
What's that you hold ? a bit of sweet wild-thyme.
Ah ! what an eloquence of memory
A scent possesses !   Dreams of boyhood come.
The scent fumes up with penetrating breath
Into dark secret cells about the brain
That only scent or sound can ever reach.
I seem again to climb with boyish zest
About the ruin yonder on the hill.
We talk of high adventure, wondrous deeds,
Of Grecian heroes, Middle Age romance,
Strange tales of magic, and Arabian Nights.
Anon we paddle, bare-legged, in the stream,
Declare the pine trees overhead are palms,
And call our schoolboy jackets coats of mail :

Or you insist on being Inca-King,
And making me Pizarro 'gainst my will :
Whilst each of us in turn, from time to time,
Suggests a speech to fit the other's part,
Where history finds an unexpected turn.

I'll shut my eyes, and dream we're boys again :
The almost godlike joy of early youth.
Steals o'er my spirit : let me clasp your hand.
Now, go—and sing that song to me—you know—
The one I wrote when you were going away.
The times are changed, and we with them indeed !
But ah ! thank God, our love is not.   But sing.

Change is for ever working round us here,
    With hill and vale, with river, shore, and tree :
Nothing that is but unto Change doth veer.
        But still, dear Friend, remain thou true to
        me :—
        Unchanged in constant Change, be true to me.

The sky is mutable with light and shade ;
    A restless heart is beating in the sea :

But though all things from what they be should fade,
 Still, still, I plead, remain thou true to me.
 Unchanged in constant Change, be true to me.

Man's hopes and customs change with every clime ;
 To altered Faiths each Age doth bow the knee :
But Love's the same for all and every time,
 And, in its name, remain thou true to me :
 Unchanged in constant Change, be true to me.

F

FAITHFUL UNTO DEATH. .

(WRITTEN FOR RECITATION.)

The following lines were written for recitation on an incident
of the Russian campaign under Napoleon in the winter
of 1812. The young Prince Emilius, of Hesse Darm-
stadt, was one of Napoleon's allies, and had led to
the field in his service a thousand of his own men.
After the burning of Moscow he shared in the terrible
retreat. Pursued by the Russians, they marched for
days through the snow-drifted forests and plains, until
of the thousand men ten alone remained. These lines
are supposed to take up the story after the men have
been wandering for days in the snow. Lord Houghton
(whose beautiful verses on this subject are well known,
but which do not lend themselves to the requirements
of the reciter) gave me the facts of the story, having
heard them, when a young man, from the lips of Prince
Emilius himself.

> On in the snow—on in the snow—
> Blinded and numbed, the soldiers go.
> With footfall silenter than theirs
> Death dogs their steps : and, unawares,

Strikes down his victims one by one,

Pursuit is distanced : doom begun.

Frost-bitten fingers, stiff with cold,

Seem frozen to the gun they hold.

The icicles hang on beard and hair ;

The breath like smoke goes out in the air :

Till reason and thought begin to wane,

And only the dull, blind sense of pain,

And the instinct of Duty till Death, remain.

On in the snow—on in the snow—

The cruel, drifting, deadly snow,—

They march in silence, with muffled tread :

Till one of them stumbles,—and drops behind, dead !

And the others shudder, and glance around—

For they hear, growing nearer, an ominous sound

In the woods—the dismal howl

Of the wolves that after them stealthily prowl.

By open waste :—by dreary wood :—

By rivers black and frozen flood—

On in the snow—on in the snow—

Ever, with thinning ranks, they go.

The Prince Emilius looked on his band,

   And his heart seemed like to break.

These were the men, who, for his sake,
Had left their Fatherland,
A thousand men in all,
To follow his bugle-call,
Three months before !—a thousand men :—
And of that thousand now he counted ten !

"Halt !" cried the Prince. The spectral band
Stood still, awaiting his command.
With tight-clenched hands Emilius stood.
Far off, a wolf howled in the wood :
And one lad, leaning on his comrade's arm,
Cried out he saw his home—the farm—
The sunny hill-slope, clothed with vine—
And heard the murmur of the Rhine !
He called his sweetheart's name, and then
Fell prone. And, looking on his men,
The Prince said,—" It is best we face
The truth. We shall not leave this place.
The end has come. God knoweth best.
To live we must have rest :—to rest
Is death. Together let us die.
See ! yonder empty hut close by :—
Thither let us repair—and sleep.

Our slumber will be long and deep !
'Tis worse than useless, further strife !
You well have borne your part in life :
Bear it in death as well.   On high
Perchance I'll rise to testify
To your unflinching loyalty.
My brothers ! though we lay us down
Defeated, and without renown,
There we shall wear the Victor's crown."
Silent they stood, and silently they heard,
They could not answer : none could speak a word.
But when, " Is it agreed ?" Emilius said,
Each man looked up at him, and bowed the head.

Then Prince Emilius went to every man,
Slim youth, or stern-browed veteran,
And kissed him, holding fast his hand :
He dared not speak lest he should be unmanned.
So, moving toward the hut, he pushed the door
Open ; then looking on them all once more,
He flung himself upon the cold earth floor.
He heard the soldiers pause outside the hut,—
They came in slowly,—then the door was shut—
And all grew still and dark as death.

Soon as they heard the deep-drawn breath
Which told them Prince Emilius slept
(For they a wakeful watch had kept),
They all rose up, and softly crept
Up toward the sleeping man.
For even in the moment's span
Ere they came in, they'd laid their plan
In hurried whispers.   Each began
To strip off coat and cloak : this done,
They placed them lightly, one by one,
Upon the young Prince lying there.
They shivered in the icy air ;
But round and over him they laid
Their own warm clothes until they made
A covering that might frost defy.
Then they crept out, all silently :
And, in the snow, beneath that freezing sky,—
Some, hand in hand,—all clustered near the door—
They laid them down, and slept—to wake no more.

The long, still hours of sleep,
Silence, and darkness deep,
Seemed frozen into endless night.
Over the sky a cold, sad light

Had turned the world to death-like gray,
When the Prince woke.   Another day !
Is it a dream ? he looks around.
Alone !—He calls :—no answer—not a sound !
How has he lived through all the night ?
And how withstood the deadly blight
Of frost as he lay there asleep.
What's this ?   He lies beneath a heap
Of cloaks and coats !   In heart and limb
He feels new life.   His senses swim,—
A sudden light breaks in on him ;
He struggles up from off the floor ;
He staggers quickly toward the door—
He bursts it open—rushes out—and lo !
The men, half naked, in the shroud-like snow.
In one swift glance he reads the truth, and then
The cry goes up,—" My men ! my faithful men !"

Faithful, and not in vain !   As if their thought
Its own fulfilment wrought
By sheer intensity and strength,
The rescue came at length.
French soldiers, ere the hour was gone,
Came past, and with them he went on.

For him thus saved the years to come
   Brought light and honour without stain ;
And shouts of welcome brought him home
   In triumph to his own again.

Yet oft, in golden summer-time,
   In his own Rhineland, when his ears
Would catch the well-remembered chime
   Of bells he knew in boyhood's years :
Or from the hillside, clothed with vine,
He saw afar the sunlight shine
Upon the waters of the Rhine ;
   His eyes would fill with sudden tears,
And he would see that hut that stood
Deep in the rugged Russian wood ;
And, by the hut One, all in white,
Upon whose brows an aureole light
   Would from the skies descend ;
   Who slowly o'er the earth would bend,
And write upon the shroud-like snow :—
" For greater love no man can show
   Than lay his life down for his friend."

A FAREWELL.

(For Recitation with Music.)

Here, where a year ago we met, Good-bye !
   Strange—that we part upon the very place,
Where, gazing on you, passionate and shy,
   I thought that Life looked at me through your face.

How I recall the ball-room's brilliant scene !
   Glitter of lights : the air with flowers made sweet :
The jewelled crowd 'mong which you moved, a queen :
   The pulse and rhythm of the dancing feet.

The memory of a valse is with me yet.
   It teaches me—though how I scarce can say—
The meaning of that strange, intense regret
   That underlies a valse, however gay.

You smiled, unconscious of the flash that burst
From out that smile, and set my heart aglow :
And still you smile, serenely, as at first :—
What shall I say ?—are you unconscious now ?

I know that I have built Love's prison well :
But has sometimes no smothered song or cry
From Love, who maddened in his silent cell,
Struck on your ears as you were passing by ?

When we have laughed, I think you must have heard
The sob that spoke of underlying tears.
And surely in the lightly-spoken word
You caught a meaning, not for other ears.

But you did not !—you did not !   Is it so ?
Well, well : if men will dream vain dreams, they must.
But it seems piteous we so seldom know
The Dead Sea apples till they turn to dust.

Now, in your queenly way, you cross the room,
To wish good fortune may my steps attend !
A year ago my heart burst into bloom
At that sweet voice :—and now ! is this the end ?

" Yes : it was bright, that night a year ago.

    Do I remember it ?—what need to tell ?

What a good valse we had that evening !—So,

    You'll not return for years ?   Good-bye—Farewell."

Ah, you sweep on ! and with the farewell breath

    You bandy words of courteous commonplace !

Well : now I know it was not Life, 'twas Death

    That looked that night upon me through your face.

Death, said I ? do I talk of dying then ?

    Folks do not die so.   Oh no, I shall live :

Life's not the only thing in mortal men

    That has the gift of Death.   " Hic jacets " give

A record of our last mortality :

    But all those unseen, unembodied things

That make life life, ah, these may die,

    And we live on : and who their requiem sings ?

Ho ! Life and Death set to a valse tune !—Yes :

    Smiles, we have oft been told, can rival sighs :

The thought is threadbare : true, though, none the less.

    There is a touch of death in all good-byes.

How you would laugh such "sentiment" to scorn.
　　I do not so : believing, without doubt,
The things that move our lives are sometimes born
　　From that same sentiment which you would flout.

The hardest, dullest life, if bared to light,
　　Would show strange dramas : and would have to own
Its roots, perhaps, lay deep, far out of sight,
　　In hopes and memories known to it alone.

Years hence, I dare say, none will guess or know
　　The last year's history, its hopes and fears :
The first line that is traced upon the brow
　　Makes little difference in a few short years!

Such lines are but dead Hope's faint signatures :
　　No one can read them—scarcely we ourselves !
But those writ by a hand as soft as yours
　　Hurt more than those which ruthless Nature delves.

A wise man said he knew no sadder sight
　　Than a child crying o'er its broken toy.
A love dream :—is it not a thing as slight
　　As any plaything made for childhood's joy?

A poor toy, broken by a touch too rough!

   A valse tune fits such childish woes to tell.

So—let it speak.   Its pathos is enough.

   It sang our Greeting : now it breathes Farewell.

A LEGEND OF CHERTSEY.

(WRITTEN FOR RECITATION.)

In the days before the king had come again to take
    his own,

When the iron will of Cromwell filled the nation's empty
    throne,

One bright summer evening,—so the story runs,—in
    Chertsey town,

As the sun in clouds of glory through the west was
    sinking down,

There were standing by the churchyard gate an old man,
    bowed with care ;

By his side a girl—the gold of sunset lighting up her hair.

"Master Noel," she was saying, "ah, you know as well
    as I,

Martin Riversdale, my lover, he to-night is doomed to
    die !

Doomed to die to-night, at sunset, when the curfew bell
    is heard :

Cromwell's coming—he might stop the fatal sentence
    with one word.

But he may not come till after they have fired the fatal
    shot.

Curfew is the signal.   Listen :—ah ! for pity, ring it not !

Wait at least a little : give us time—time till the General
    come.

See, the people gathering yonder :—hark ! I hear the
    muffled drum.

Wait—delay ! and I will bless you with my latest, dying
    breath :

Every moment that we gain is weighted now with life
    and death."

Then the sexton answered, sadly : " Ah ! you know not
    what you ask.

For these forty years to ring that curfew bell hath been
    my task.

Not a single night I've missed in all these strange,
    eventful times.

Still my life hath wrought its fashion to that tower and
    to those chimes.

I have known you from a child, dear: you and Martin:
    loved you too:
But a duty lies before me, and that duty I must do.
I am deaf, and old, and broken; and the sadder for this
    day:
I can scarcely hear your words, dear, but I know what
    you would say.
Let me face my duty bravely—face it—whatsoe'er it be!
Go, my child: no, leave me.—In this I am worse than
    deaf to thee."

Silent stands the girl: the sunset hides the pallor of her
    brow.
In her heart, heroic purpose quickens into action now.
In the morning she had heard the Judge the fatal
    sentence pass:—
" Martin Riversdale, 'tis proven that you worshipped at
    High Mass,
Held at daybreak on the Lord's Day, in the Chapel of
    the Hall:—
You refuse the names of those then present—popish
    traitors all!
Wherefore this the sentence is—that, when the curfew
    bell shall toll,

You be shot to-night, at sunset.—Heaven have mercy on
    your soul."

And she left the courthouse calmly, but with face a
    deadly white :

And she heard the townsfolk saying, " Martin will be
    shot to-night,

When they ring the bell at sundown," and had kept a
    silent tongue :

For her heart was whispering, " Courage ! and that bell
    shall not be rung !"

She remembered how, in childhood, she and Martin
    oftentimes

Had climbed up the old, dark belfry, and had watched
    the ringing chimes :

For they loved the good old sexton, and he often let
    them play

Up and down the quaint old belfry, with its stairways
    dark and gray.

Well she knew their every turning, to the topmost dizzy
    stair :

Often she had climbed to gather wild flowers that had
    rooted there.

Now, in these faint, childish memories she a hope of
    rescue saw :

Desperate ! but at such a desperate time she clung to it
    the more.

"Go, my child," the old man said.   "Ah ! would that
    I could give you strength.

Though the day be ne'er so long it rings to evensong at
    length.

Go, and pray : and close your ears, lest you should hear
    the fatal bell,

And the volley that will echo it, with fiercer, deadlier knell.

You and he have often played about my knees, ah !
    woe's the day !

Helped me open yonder door ; cheered me with your
    childish play !

Would that I had died before, and ne'er had seen this
    morning's light !

I will lift my heart in prayer the while I ring that bell
    to-night."

Then she left him : for a moment hid—then darted
    toward the door :

Slid the bolt, and entered ; she had loosed the wooden
    bar before.

Like a ghost on the dark stairway, but with heart with
    love made bold,

Up she mounts, past lancet windows, by the stairs she
    knew of old.

On and upward—on and upward : in the darkness—not
    a sound !

Higher—higher : dusty arches—slippery stairways, round
    and round !

On she presses—on and upward—till she sees a ray of
    light,—

Struggles on another moment, and then gains the top-
    most height.

Through the windows of the belfry she can see the town
    below ;—

Houses, meadows, winding river, and the sunset's crimson
    glow :—

On the buttress grows the wild flower : in a high and
    dark recess

Hangs the fatal bell that soon will ring her lover's doom,
    unless——

Ah ! what is her thought ?   How can she stop its ring-
    ing—make it dumb ?

See ! she watches, watches, watches, till the fatal moment
come !

Now—now !—see—the rope is moving ! and the bell
begins to sway !

In a moment it will give voice, and all hope be swept away !

Courage !—one wild leap :—she grasps the bell:—it lifts
her off the ground :

To and fro it sways—but dumbly—for her hands have
hushed the sound.

Swinging, swinging :—meadows, houses, winding river,
sunset's glow

Swim before her as she hangs there, and the bell moves
to and fro !

Swinging, swinging :—hands are bleeding, sense is failing
with the pain :—

Still she clings, and still she clings on, clinging still with
might and main !

And the sexton, deaf, and with his heart absorbed in
prayer, below

Pulls the rope, nor hears, nor cares to hear, its answering
note of woe !

Lo ! the swinging lessened—ceased ! She slipped, with
sobbings, to the floor,

Where, a happy child, she oft had played with Martin
    years before !

There she lay, half dead, and fainting ; whilst low down
    the western sky,

Like a fire the broad sun blazed : and in the prison-yard,
    hard by,

Stood her lover, ready, waiting for the curfew bell to
    sound :

Whilst the poor, half-frightened people, pale and trem-
    bling, gathered round.

There they waited, still expectant. Some have gone
    toward the church tower,

Wondering why the curfew still delays to ring the sunset
    hour :—

When—in silence—hark ! a distant bugle peals across
    the land :—

Up the street a man comes spurring, —" Cromwell !
    Cromwell is at hand !"

And the girl, who down the belfry stairs had crept, and
    reached the gate,

Heard. the shout, and hurried onward, lest her prayer
    should come too late.

And, before 'twas found the sexton deemed that he had
    rung the bell,

She was at the feet of Cromwell—there she pleaded long
    and well :—

There she showed her trembling hands, by the iron and
    woodwork torn :—

Told how Martin only bore the Faith his fathers long
    had borne :—

Prayed for pardon :—spoke of Mercy, Mercy that is
    throned above :—

Pleaded with the noble and heart-moving eloquence of
    Love :—

Till the iron heart was melted. "Let his life," he said,
    "be spared !

Love must greatly claim our reverence, when thus greatly
    hath it dared.

Almost seems the sun to answer, and delay its course
    to-night :

Let no curfew ring its setting, for we do not miss its
    light

When such faithfulness is shining in our midst with
    goodly ray.

You have saved your lover's life : go—seek him : tell
    him what I say :—

Let him give his life in answer—and give both to God
    this day !

On to Chertsey. Let us enter with a psalm upon
our lip ;

Finding in this deed of love, which all can honour,
fellowship.

Tell the story to your children : and their children still
shall tell

How the Maiden conquered Time, and hushed the
ringing of the Bell."

THE HOUR BEFORE THE DAWN.[1]

(For Recitation with Music.)

Scene, a room, dimly lighted with a shaded lamp. Flowers
 on the tables. A large bow-window, with the curtains
 drawn. A piano, with sheets of music piled upon it.
 In an arm-chair a young man is seated. At his side
 stands his mother, with her hand upon his shoulder.
 He turns to her, kisses her hand, and says :—

LEAVE me, dear mother : go—and have no fear.
    I shall be happy here until the morn,
Nor want for aught. You see the bell is near.
    Go, rest : you look so pale,—so tired and worn !
Leave me awhile : I like to be alone.
    Put back the lamp :—and let the blind be drawn

---

[1] I am indebted for the leading idea of these lines to Mr. A.
F. Westmacott.

Aside :—With stars the skies are sown.

    Open the window.   Place those flowers near.

    Mother, your love has never seemed so dear.

    Good-night.   Yes—leave me, mother, till the dawn.

She goes.   I hear the faltering footsteps stay

Outside the door, as loth to pass away.

She longs to stay beside me all the night.

'Tis late already : for the lamp's dim light

Has flickered low : and in the east afar,

Surely that star must be the morning star.

But all the world seems very still and calm.

No earliest bird pipes yet its matin psalm.

The air is breathless ! not a leaf astir !

The tenderest chords of sense grow tenderer

At such an hour : and influences wake

That sleep by day.   They rule the night, and make

An hour like this their own.   The eye and ear

Strain for some sound of moving life around :—

The world is sleeping both to sight and sound.

The perfume of a hundred dew-drenched flowers

Hangs in the air.   From the far Abbey towers

The quarters chime.   I hear them clearly borne
Through the mute air.   Is it so near the morn?
Three hours since midnight!   Is the time so close
When the faint east will flush with gold and rose?
No sign as yet that night's veil is withdrawn!
It is that darkest hour before the dawn.

What is this restlessness that makes me fret,
And fills me with unspeakable regret?
Dear Art! my Better Self!—I turn to thee.
   Strengthen and calm me, as thou oft hast done.
For Failure thou hast naught of cruelty:
   Only for Fame and Praise that have been won
By degradation of thy majesty.
   Hast thou the scornful and rejecting hand.
Comfort thy weak, but not unfaithful son:
   Send me some message from thine Unseen Land.
Let me forget my petty griefs and strife,
And all the dark entanglements of life,
In thy eternal calm and loveliness.
   Pour light upon me.   Let me hear
   The music of thy presence.   Ah, draw near
And nearer as the world grows less and less.

I long to hear some chord, some note, some strain.
There's music here within me—and 'twere vain
To echo *that*—but yet I long to hear
The air vibrate with actual sound.   'Tis near—
The instrument !—I long to touch the keys ;
And wake once more familiar harmonies.
The sound in this deep silence will gain power :
The time, the solemn spirit of the hour,
Will hallow every note to blessedness :
Till hearing, linked with memory, grow scarce less
Than worship ; and the very heart be drawn
Upward and outward to the coming dawn.

'Twill wake my mother.   Nay : if she's asleep,
Her wearied sleep will be too dense and deep.
If she be waking, she will hear the chords,
And they will summon her like spoken words.
Better : for in their message she will read,
The dawn is coming to my life indeed.
Weak ! I am weak.   I scarce can guide my limbs
    Toward the beloved instrument—though near.
The room looks strange and far away.   It swims
    Before me as I move.   Ah friend ! so dear—

So loved !   Again I touch the keys : my hands
Are feeble to obey my will's commands :
They wander into discords : but the song
Pours life into my veins, and I grow strong.
The joy is almost more than I can bear !
Music ! ah, who thy message may declare,
The limits of thy sovereignty define,
Or prophesy the future that is thine ?

    Latest born of all the Arts,
       Welcome to thy golden reign :
    All the joy of youth is thine !
       Earth in thee grows young again.
    Tell us all we ever felt ;
       Every scene our life has known.
    Sing to us : and let our hearts
       Give the echo to each tone.
    Music !—ah, the very word
       Seems in fire and glory writ :
    Crowned by poets, lit with love,
       Heaven itself hath promised it.
    Hearts that throb, and swell, and yearn
       With a poetry that's mute :—
    Lives that suffer :—thoughts that burn :—
       Hopes that bud, but fail of fruit :—

Poems which are sung in silence,
   Unrecorded and unheard :—
Joys and dreams that have no answer :—
   Love that passes without word :—
Whispers from the worlds beyond us :—
   Echoes from the lives gone by :—
Voices of Life's eager questions :—
   Mysteries of Death's reply :—
Find an utterance and a meaning,
   Read a far off mystic sign,
Hear a promise of fulfilment,
   Music, in some voice of thine !

I see once more my Past from childhood's hour,
   The flattering dreams of triumph yet to be :
I feel again the young belief in power,
   The hope that called itself a prophecy.
Such hopes to natures that are strong and true
Are prophecies indeed and lead them on
To high endeavour and achievement too.
Whose was the fault then that those hopes but shone
So fitfully for me ?   What did I lose ?
Where fail ?—when called upon in life to choose.
Chose I a wrong path, or a hopeless aim ?

Ah ! shall I give my failure its right name ?
'Tis here—in these hands that had no strength for strife,
No grasp upon the ruggedness of life :—
Here—on these feet that tripped at every stone,
And would not tread the path of work alone :—
Here—on the heart and brain that surely knew
The Artist's sympathy, and passion too,
To see and feel, but not the power to do !
These hands ! and might they not the' strength have
    gained
To fight as all have fought who have attained
Prizes in life ? who knows ?   Once in them lay
A hand, smaller and softer far than they :
Smaller and softer—yet it gave them strength
Such as might well have gained for them at length
The prizes they have missed without it.   Yes :—
They found a purpose in that soft caress,
Lost soon as found.   For though it was so much
To me, and nerved me with its very touch,
It found no answer in my clasping hand :
No answer it, at least, could understand,
Or cared to read.   White hand, you were too sweet,
Too dainty far for mine.   My pulses beat
Remembering you.   I wonder, do you know

That they are beating for you, though so low?
What folly! Nay, white hand, to you 'twas naught—
A merest waft of girlhood's waking thought:
You're happy now, clasped in a loving hold.
There was no blame—the tale has oft been told;
What shall we call it?—a mistake—that's all:
Reality to one, and what you call
A dream, remembered with a smile almost,
Unto the other. Mistakes like that have cost
More than my life has in't to give ere this.
No blame! Love sometimes asks for one brief kiss,
Your life:—and passes on, without a sigh.
There is no blame; for, of a certainty,
There seems no choice:—we pay the price and die,
Knowing the cost! I do not blame—not I!
White hand, I love you still, and wish you well.
When you touched mine how could your heart foretell
The touch would wake the one chord that is true
To life in me?—'Twere mute still, save for you.
But for that waking, though the music be
The faintest echo of that melody,
That is to life as sunshine to the land,
I thank you and I love you, gentle hand!
The opening song was sweet beyond all words;

Rich as, in June, the carols of the birds
Fluted at sunrise, on a woodland lawn,
When all the world is flooded with the dawn !

The Dawn !—ah, see ! The clouds have seen the sun,
And quicken into glory one by one.
A sense of wakening life is in the trees—
A flutter as of wings !   Soft harmonies
Awake to answer those the eyes
Receive in colour from the flushing skies.
The old familiar scene looks new and strange,
As though I need had seen it truly.   Change !
But in the eyes that look, not in the place.
Mother !—I'm glad you're here.   Your well-loved face
It too has something in it strange and new.
Why did you come ?   I did not call for you—
But I am glad.   You see I could not stand
Against temptation.   Let me be—My hand
Clings to the keyboard.   I am happy here,
Feeling that both of you, so loved, are near.
Place your arms round me : kiss me on the brow.
The sun is shining full upon us now.
So—let me play :—yes, yes—I will !   I'm strong.
Would I could greet the Dawn with worthier song !

But 'tis the notes themselves—the very chords—
I love—They ease me more than any words.
Ah ! think not that I lack in reverence
At such a time.   But I would go out hence
Hearing this voice of music, which has been
The master-chord in life to me.   "Twould seem
A different revelation comes to each :
To every listening ear there is a speech
That comes to it with glory and a sign,
And best may spell for it the Name Divine :
And music seems the speech that speaks to mine.
If you should see her—tell her—tell her this,
That in my life the fairest memory is
The day I met her : and that, just before,—
Before—the Dawn (the sun shines more and more !)
I played the air she liked—the air I wrote
For her.   Ah ! how I stumble at each note !
My fingers seek the melody in vain :—
'Tis gone—ah no—I have it now again.
Say now the words you taught me at your knee :
They touch the very heart of Melody.
These sounds of mine will soon in silence sink :
Their music will not ever cease, I think.

THE LOVER.

ABATE, O nightingale, thy passionate lay,
　　Or by a voice it will be put to shame :—
Fade, stars ; or soon your lustre will give way
　　Before a glance in which the heart takes flame.

I scarcely heed the beauty that I see ;
　　My heart is reigning even in my eyes :
And joyous Love arising, winged, and free,
　　Compels the earth, and treads the very skies.

The stars are nothing to me when I gaze
　　Into the heaven of that loving smile :—
You speak to me :—and never word of praise
　　Sweet Philomel can gain from me the while.

The Beauty round me, howsoe'er intense,
   Seems but fit setting for Love's rich delight :
A part of joy so high that every sense
   Must be fulfilled to enter on that height.

Sing, nightingales !   Be minstrels to our Feast :
   Shine out, O stars ! as torches to our Throne :—
Come, Earth, from North to South, from West and East,
   And Love shall make your Beauty all his own.

IN ILLNESS.

Over and over and over again,
In and out, and about, the brain,
All the day long, all the day long,
Something has sung me an unknown song.
Is there anything near me, afloat in the air?
Is there anything standing behind my chair ;—
And is that its breath at the roots of my hair?
I have heard that the gleam of the Crotalus' eyes
Works such wicked and baleful sorceries,
That its victim, bewitched and with freezing breath
Stands waiting the rattle and poison of death ;
Whilst with flattening head, the accursed thing
Unwindeth its coils for the fatal spring.
So seem I to wait :—whilst all through the brain,
Over, and over, and over again,
Windeth that strange and mysterious strain,

Windeth and coileth, till every sense
Seems drawn to the utmost, quivering, tense,
Drawn by the magnet-like spell of the song,
Drawn into listening all the day long.—

It comes with whispers and murmurings,
With the trampling of feet, and the beating of wings,
And a sense of the approach of invisible things,
With splendours that grow from, and sink into gloom,
With the glare of a crisis, and the shade of a doom ;—
It fills me with grief lest its rhythm should die
Ere I fashion the shape of its melody :—
Now seems it to swell, and grow higher and higher,
With a roar and a crash, like a wind-angered fire ;
Till I, knowing it coming, and hearing it come,
Could scream, were I held not passive and dumb :—
And now with a sudden plunge and sigh,
It dives in the wells of memory ;
And where the sad waters lie darkling in night,
It shoots cruel shafts of irreverent light ;
Till faces forgotten, and happier years,
Youth's joys and mistakes, dead Hopes and Fears,
Drowned deep in regret, and bitter with tears,
Seem to stir into something like life again,

At the incantation of that refrain ;—
Till my eyes are brimming, and all grows dim,
As the cadence of that mysterious hymn
Falleth and riseth with the breast,
Riseth and falleth, and will not rest,
But winds through the heart and coils round the brain,
Over and over and over again.

Yet I know that the room is silent all :
For a denser stillness begins to fall,
As the gloomy twilight, drenched in rain,
Is darkened, and drawn from the window-pane.
The fire, whose vivid and comforting glow
Has cheered me, is glimmering, fitful and low ;
So dull that the shadowy walls of the room
Have vanished beyond the contracting gloom.
There is not a sound, save, now and again,
A desolate plash from the falling rain ;
A bell that is tolling far away ;
And a cinder that clinks as it turns to gray.

And here I sit in the great armchair,
And in me, and round me, everywhere,
With a growing sense of crisis and pain.

Over and over and over again,
In the same mysterious time and tone,
Repeated, and yet never known,
Just as I've heard it all day long,
I can feel the swing of that terrible song.

I wish that some one would come in to me :
The sound of a cheery voice, maybe
Would somehow set things all aright.
I wish that some one would come with a light.
I shall madden here alone, in the dark,
Whilst the fire is fading out, spark by spark.
Till the last red flame gives its dying start,
And sinks back dull and faint and dead ;
And that evil song is still at my heart,
And coiling itself about my head,
Winding in and about the brain.
Over and over and over again.

* * * * *

A DEAD LOVE'S OBSEQUIES.

CHOOSE me a lonely and desolate spot,
    Bitter with blight, and canker accurst;
Where human footstep echoes not,
    And untamed Nature worketh her worst.
Let the toad croak loud, and the snake slip by,
    While the raven flappeth his wing above :—
And straightway I to that place will hie,
    For such is the place for thy burial, Love.

Choose me a dark and terrible night,
    When Death is about i' the murky air :
When children shriek in their sleep for fright,
    And strong men cross themselves in prayer :
Let the wind wail loud over city and kirk,
    And the thunderbolt crash from the cloud above ;
And then I will get me straight to my work,
    For such is the time for thy burial, Love.

And choose you a funeral garment to wear,
    And write me a fitting funeral song,
For you must be Priest and Mourner there,
    And chant me a psalm as we go along.
And why? The Love I shall bury that night,
    Is the corpse of the Love you gave to me :
'Tis meet that I bury it deep out of sight,
    And 'tis meet that you should be by to see.

For thus, as whilst yet it lived, its face
    To us, to us twain only, was known ;
So now it is dead, its resting-place
    Shall be known to none but us alone.
And the place is here, and the time is now :—
    Hush ! Nay, it is useless to weep or rave !
I give you one last kiss on the brow.—
    My God ! it is done. Let Love rot in its grave.

ALONE.

In the quiet summer evening,
You and I. beside the window,
Look upon the happy landscape :
        Lonely, each; though hand in hand.

Boys are bathing in the river ;
I can hear their joyous voices,
As they swim in lustrous water,
        Round the golden meadowland.

From the hayfields, home-returning,
Troop the reapers by the waggon ;
All the sounds of life and labour
        Change to music in the air.

Far away, the bells are ringing :
Through the evening's dreamy splendour
They come pealing, with a pathos
      That no language can declare.

Earth is very fair and joyous :
And to us the hour is blessed,—
Blessed in each other's presence,
      And in thought of days gone by.

Yet I feel the hot tears rising ;
And in your eyes tears are shining ;—
But you cannot tell me wherefore,
      Neither can I tell you why.

Unto you and me this moment
Speaks, no doubt, a different message ;
Speaks to each, for each one only,
      What none else could understand.

I can only call you " Dearest !"
You can only say " I love you !"
All beyond is self and silence :—
      Lonely, each : though hand in hand.

TO CALMNESS.

Sing thou to me, my heart,
    For I am vexed and weary :
Be psalmist to thyself,
    Take up thy harp, and cheer me.
Sing unto me of calmness, fair and strong,
Until she come to me upon your song.

Why am I sad to-night ?
    Is it a thing so strange,
To see life's colours fade,
    And find that friends can change ?
That Will at times seems come to cope with Fate ?
That he who longs to do, but learns to wait ?

Calmness ! oh me—that word
    So often on our lips,

When lights that lead our lives
    Are shadowed in eclipse !
Divinest calmness—come to me to-night,
And fill my spirit with thine equal light.

Ay, thou for whom my soul
    Doth daily, hourly pray ;
Oh hardest maid to win,
    And soonest scared away—
Come ! come and clasp me in thy cold, chaste arms :
Passionless, chant me thy strong-hearted psalms.

RE-UNITED.

Whilst you were far away, Life seemed
   A restless slumber naught could break.
I did not live : I only dreamed :
   But you return—and I awake !

Thrice welcome to the blessed day !
   The sun is shining :—all is new !
The sun ?—the morning, do I say ?
   The light I welcome shines from you.

Yes : like a dream from off my brain,
   The motley days of Absence fly :
I wake.—I take up life again.—
   Was it last night you said " Good-bye " ?

THE day will come to us again ;
   The summer will return :
The frozen streamlet gush afresh
   Amidst the new-grown fern.
The fallow harvest-fields next year
   Their golden robes will don ;—
But ah ! the love you bore me once
   Is gone—is gone—is gone !

There's nothing—nothing in the world
   Can give it life again :
No bribe of joy, no gift of tears,
   No sacrifice of pain :—
Nor word, nor deed, nor prayer, nor threat,
   Nor smile, nor agony,
Nor life, nor death, nor heaven itself
   Can bring it back to me.

Ambition conquers oft defeat ;
 Hope hath eternal breath :
Faith knows a more than Phœnix life ;
 And Truth is freed from Death.
Our souls will live again when life
 Hath passed from earth away ;
But ah ! for love that once is dead
 There is no Easter Day.

Seed-time and harvest will return ;
 Earth will retrieve her scars :
The day-time will renew his songs ;
 The night regain her stars :
The sun will shine on us again
 As bright as e'er it shone :
But ah ! the love you bore me once
 Is gone—is gone—is gone !

IN SORROW.

The trivial incidents of every day
    Drive home the meaning of the mourner's loss :
We trip upon a briar in the way,
    And thereon feel how heavy is the cross.

The strongest recollections seem to lie,
    Like latent music, in the commonest things :
We put our hand upon them, passing by,
    And rudely touch the unsuspected strings.

And lo ! there rises up an awful song—
    The passion and the pathos of dead years !
Harmonious minors, sweeping full and strong,
    And sapping all our strength with rush of tears.

I

ROUGE ET NOIR.

(Written for Recitation.)

I had lost all night, with ill-fortune so strange,
That I said with each venture, "The luck will change."
Every night, as you know, has repeated the tale :
The fever that heightens, the hopes that fail.
I tell you my all was placed on the stake.
Well—I lost. And I knew that the morning would break
On my hopeless ruin, disgrace, despair,
Unless Fortune changed. And, bribed by what prayer,
Or compelled by what curse, would she deign to show
One glimpse of the light that a year ago
Led me on and on with such certain flame,
Till it changed in one hour to darkness and shame?

I played on : till the bells from the church tolled four.
Then I knew,—though I saw of the dawn no more

Than here and there through a curtain's fold
A narrow streak of luminous gold,—
That the latest gleam of the morning star
Had gone out in the rose of the east afar.
And I thought that a shame seemed to pass o'er the
    room :
And the lights grew more sickly, and denser the gloom ;
And the people looked strange ; and I scarce knew
    my face
In the mirror beside, as I turned from my place
To a sofa, and sank on its cushions, and lay,
And thought that my senses were falling away.
Fritz passed me and spoke, but my tongue seemed tied.
Then he drew the dark velvet curtains aside,
Flung the lace from the window, and opened it wide.
And with holiness far above insult or taint,
Like the glory that haloes the face of a saint,
Heavenly, pure, unsullied, bright,
Flowed in a blue flood of morning light.
The air was cool as mountain rills,
And fresh with the odours of meadows and hills :
On my forehead it blew, and it lifted my hair ;
(I thought that *her* fingers were wandering there.)
And I felt a waft of the unstained joy

That I used to feel, when, a light-hearted boy,
I would wake on just such a summer dawn,
And hear the thrush sing on the garden lawn ;
And dream of how happy my life should be,
Whilst the sun rose over the distant sea.
And lo ! even then, as I trembled and felt
My whole spirit burn, and begin to melt
In the morning's holy and ardent light,
A gloom and a fire passed over my sight.
For I heard, through the tumult and stir of the
      room,
Those words of madness,—those words of doom,—
Those words that so bitterly well I knew,—
" Faites votre jeu, messieurs, faites votre jeu !"
And again I felt the blackening pall
Of their magic and glamour around me fall ;
And again my better nature gives way
Before their irresistible sway ;
As, with desperate calm, I again take my place,
For the last, last time, at the long green baize,
With the sense of a fiend, hue and cry, on my track,
And the whole world a-dazzle with red and black,
Whilst I mutter under my quickening breath,—
" You make your game now for life or death !"

There are pale faces round me, and eyes that glare :
And the glitter of sconces that flicker and flare ;—
There are shuddering wafts of the morning air ;—
There is chinking of money here and there ;—
A hush around, and a storm within ;—
And the thought—Rouge ?   Noir ?—" Rouge !" God !
    will it win ?—
Then a moment that lies on the spirit like lead,
Till it burst like a thunderbolt over my head,
" Rouge perde !" and I   stagger and   fall   like   one
    dead.

Ah, yes : they tell me I fell with a scream.
It all seems now like some hideous dream.
But ah ! no dream is the ruin I face,
In all its grim, cold commonplace !
No dream was the barrel pressed on my brow
When you came and snatched it away just now !
You say there is hope even yet : if I raise
My eyes, and work toward better days,
With " never too late "—and the rest of the phrase.
Ah ! friend : do not let me blame or fret,—
Perhaps you are right,—but yet—and yet !—
My life rises up at me whilst I speak,

With a voice like the wind's, and the whirlwind's shriek :
And no accents of Hope can I hear on its blast,
No voice but the voice of the pitiless past !
The irreparable past ! with its bloodhound breath,
And with eyes that are keen as the eyes of death :—
That terrible monster of Frankenstein
That is made from a past and a nature like mine !
God help any man who tangles his life,
And slips from the plain highroads in the strife !
For whether he knowingly turns astray,
Or wanders in ignorance away,
The price must be paid—the end is the same :
And the higher the nature, the deeper the shame.
The men who keep to paths direct,
Whose ways are safe and circumspect,—
(God knows ! they too may have had to atone
For slips that to none but themselves are known,
For the heart knows its bitterness alone),—
They never can know of the hopeless maze
That hedges the wanderer in lost ways ;
That closes round him on every side ;
Where any chance of return is denied ;
Where choice of road there is none—there is none !
And whence there is no gate, no issue—but one !

Now, good-bye : yes, farewell : for our roads lie apart ;—
You're my friend, my brother ; worn here—" heart of
    heart,"—
I can trust your love always.   Now drink we a draught.
To the glad long ago—a last Brüderschaft !
So,—your arm pressing mine gives a life to the wine.
Now you must go your way—and I ?—I will go mine.

A DREAM OF LIFE.

Lo! I see children round the firelight :
   Outside the night is still, and dark and deep :
Inside, although at times the glow is bright,
   Are sounds of those who sit in gloom and weep.

Some strain their eyes into the dark afar,
   Pressing pale faces on the breath-filmed glass :
Or ask the others if they see a star :
   Or say that ghostlike figures flit and pass.

One, creeping up to where the light is strong,
   Foldeth his arms about a little maid :
And one is trying hard to sing a song
   Pretending that he does not feel afraid.

Here, sits a child who rocks himself and cries:
  There, one hangs pictures o'er the window-pane:
These laugh and dance, with wild and startled eyes:
  Those mend their broken toys, that break again.

And outside all in utter darkness lies—
  No sound—no form—no message and no sign?
Only the silence of the far-off skies:
  And stars that through the darkness calmly shine.

SUNDAY EVENING.

THE sun is setting.   By the churchyard stile,
Here on the upland, let me rest awhile.
The hour and place are beautiful to me
In seen delight and unseen memory.

The hill-slope faces westward : and the land,
Garden-like, stretches out on every hand,
And far across the meadows, golden green,
The spires of Oxford crown the lovely scene.

How the eye dwells on every landmark round!
And how the ear drinks in each pleasant sound !
Both sight and sound alike grow doubly fair,
Translated through the golden evening air.

'Tis but a few short years since here I stood,
Seeing the self-same field and hill and wood :
When, just as now, the sunset lingered low,
O'er Oxford's "crown of towers," and Isis' flow.

Often I hither walked on summer eves,
Or when October touched the yellowing leaves :
When days were drawn to longest span in June,
Or when snow shone beneath December's moon.

Dear and familiar is this twilight scene :—
That old stone tower : those yew trees, darkly green.
How well I knew the lane up which I came !
Nothing is changed, yet nothing is the same.

Nothing is changed : yet change is everywhere :—
All things the same : yet not the things they were :—
Pathetically different all appears
From this same scene as known in earlier years.

Where is the change? and what has taken flight ?
Is it the loss of that mysterious light
Which surely once upon my pathway shone :
And which I woke one day to find was gone?

Gone !—when and where I cannot tell in truth :
Gone ! ere I felt it going, with my youth !
Leaving behind for evermore a sense
Of aching void, and cureless difference.

Ah ! most pathetic of all human woe :
Tritest of sorrow that this world doth know :
Foolish to others—but to us so sore—
That wild regret for days that are no more !

What, then, does all this yearning sadness mean ?
The touching beauty of this evening scene ?
There must be answer, which some day will come,
There must be answer, though earth seems so dumb.

Once, ere my life had asked, reply seemed clear :
Now that my life has asked, no voice I hear !
No voice that speaks with any certain trust ;
None, save the Love that hopes in spite of Dust.

None, more than this—the thought that haunts the
        brain—
And whispers that its breath is not in vain :—
That somewhere will the best our life hath known
Be brought again with joy unto its own :—

That as all light has one great heart of light,
So all the things that make life fair and bright,
And noble, spring from one Eternal Root
Of which they are the flower and the fruit.

Oh for the faith of childhood, when my eyes
Saw heaven with all its angels in the skies!
Ere yet unveiling life had shown its form,
Or Thought or Passion raised their earliest storm.

Moments like these a smile of scorn may bring
To those too wise, or dull, to feel their sting :
But unto many, from such moment's strife,
Are born the thoughts that mould their afterlife.

Heart-rending sorrows, Love's awaking kiss,
These teach us most what living really is :
The heart gives fuller wisdom than the brain :
And Reason learns of passion and of pain.

So unto such as I, these moments—weak
Although they seem to those who sift and seek,
And have the power their own clear thought to tell—
Have yet their meaning, and their use as well.

Surely the tears with which my eyes are wet
Are made of something more than mere regret :
Rise from the heart's least desecrated source,
And not without some blessing take their course.

Hark ! they are singing in the church.   The hymn
Peals through the open doorway, dark and dim :
And it fulfils with more than speaking power
The loveliness and meaning of the hour.

Ah ! let me join, although with alien voice,
In that sweet hymn, that, sung by happy boys,
Where thro' the chancel steals the sun's last ray,
Touches me more than any words can say.

For such the hymn that whilst I yet was young
In school and college chapel oft I sung :
It comforted my father's wearied ears ;
And it is hallowed by my mother's tears.

Abide with me : fast falls the eventide—
To-night the well-known words seem glorified :
Embodying more, and with a voice more fine,
My inmost need, than any words of mine.

Rough were the hand such thoughts would sweep away;
Shallow the heart that did not feel their sway :
And he for whom no memories haunt the words
Is deaf to one of life's most tender chords.

O well-loved scene ! Ah, lovely summer night !
What is your message ? Who shall read aright ?
I cannot hear : for life has dulled my ears :
I cannot read ; my eyes are full of tears.

Here let me kneel, and turn me to the West,
For doubt and yearning hold my struggling breast :
And I, in reverence, would place my hand
On what the wisest cannot understand.

Hushed is the hymn : and as I westward gaze
The sun withdraws the latest of his rays.
The rooks stream home. The church clock gives the
    hour.
The far-off city answers. Spire and tower

Take up the tale. The air-wave on its swell
Brings silvery chimes, and many a deep-toned bell.
Now all is still again. The golden glow
Is fading as I reach the lane below.

THOU aw'st my soul, O Nature, most
　　When thou art robed in flowers :
The song I least am nerved to hear
　　Thou sing'st in summer hours.

The Ages pass : and never mark
　　Upon thy brows they set ;
I see no memories in thine eyes :
　　Thy voice knows no regret.

I fear 'Thee when, 'mid blight and death,
　　'Thou tak'st a ruthless way :
But ah ! my soul grows dumb with awe
　　To hear thee laugh at play.

A SUMMER NIGHT.

LISTEN and look ! How beautiful it is !
   So calm, the moon alone appears to move.
The year will know no sweeter hour than this :
   It seems to catch the spirit of our love.

The stars will hardly triumph o'er the West
   Before the East disputes their quiet reign :
The last bird scarce have fluttered to its rest,
   Before the earliest wakes to song again.

And as heart beats to heart, and hand clasps hand.
   A godlike sympathy to us is given,
With everything that lives in sea and land,
   And everything that loves in earth and heaven.

K

A STORM.

THERE is a tumult in the sea to-night !
   I see the sheeted foam flash ghastly-pale :
Whilst flakes of foam and wreaths of sea-weed dank
   Fly past me, as I lean against the gale.
The gulls are screaming in the crannied cliffs :
   And angry voices rise, that speak to me
Of giant boulder, bedded rock, and sand,
   Wrestling in agony against the sea.

There is a tumult in my heart to-night !
   The sea of passion, white with inward strife,
Uplifts its waves, and madly beat the rocks
   Where lie the very roots of Love and Life.
Its Titan strength besieges all my heart ;
   Whence issue voices wild, that speak to me
Of grappling Will, Endeavour and Resolve,
   Wrestling in agony against the sea.

Shriek, winds; and hurl the vast Atlantic waves
    In thunderpeals against the granite wall:
The throned rocks, unmoved, will face the dawn,
    And from their iron seats defy you all.
God! will the dawn behold my Will rock-firm
    From out the stress of this tumultuous fray?—
Or lying drowned in wells of deep defeat,—
    Pounded to dust—clean gone—and washed away?

AN IMPRESSION.

THE dusk of a dull November day :—
   A quiet London square :—
A line of gas-lamps in the gray,
   Blurred with the smoky air :—

A narrow strip of sunset sky,
   Seen through a leafless tree :—
The hum and drone of the streets near by,
   Like the voice of a distant sea.

And as I counted the clock strike five,
   And sat by the fire in my chair,
An old street organ began to give
   Its voice to the quiet square.

'Twas a well-known melody from one
    Of Verdi's operas ;
Where you feel the warmth of a southern sun,
    And the glow of the southern stars.

Alas ! to be worthy a poet's rhyme,
    And to have its touch of romance,
It should have been on the "castled Rhine,"
    Or some old-world town of France.

It should have been my lady's song
    In an old oak-panelled hall :
Or the strain from a gondola floating along :
    Or the hymn from a convent wall.

But dull were the things I saw and heard :—
    Yet it was not these alone :—
For a pathos for which I have no word
    Had made them all its own.

I had held my sorrow from giving way
    Through months of pent-up care :
But the song in the dusk of that wintry day
    Mastered me then and there.

NEW YEAR'S NIGHT.

Just as I gained my doorstep in the snow,
   And paused a moment, looking toward the sky,
The stroke of midnight sounded, solemn, slow;
   And bells began to ring out merrily.

And suddenly I saw the well-known place
   With other eyes,—the same, yet not the same!
The whole world changed before my very face
   With change that knows no form, and has no name.

Something ne'er seen before rose into sight;
   Something, to come back never, went out hence:
Yet nothing warned me that that New Year's night
   Would touch my life with such strange difference.

I heard the bells go ringing, far and near ;
   Over the way the rooms were brightly lit :
A window was thrown open wide to hear ;
   Across the light I saw dark shadows flit :—

Above, the frosty stars were sparkling keen ;
   The wheel-ruts furrowed the discoloured snow :—
There was no inch of the familiar scene,
   No sound or echo, that I did not know.

Yet all was seen and heard for the first time ;
   Almost by one new-born, as it might be :—
Many New Years since then have rung the chime ;
   But that New Year has never ceased for me.

ON CHARLTON HILL.

I LOOKED to London when the sun was low,
And watched the river as it curved away
To where St. Paul's, against the after-glow
Rose o'er the masts, and fog-banks dull and gray.
Mournful it was to watch the river glide
Between the mud-banks of the ebbing tide :
Mournful the hush !—The city lay too far
To send its voices thither : yet too near
For earth-born, natural sounds to greet the ear.
Dim through the smoke-drift burnt the evening star.
And as I stood and dreamed a moment there,
I wished that Earth were once more young and fair,
And Progress looked but dingy, dull and vain,
Beside the vision of Pan's golden reign.

IN WESTMINSTER ABBEY.

Time, who unmakes us all, hath made thee strong !
The Past is living still thine aisles among,
To tell in word, and symbolism high,
How much there is in life that cannot die.
Here let me gaze with reverent eyes around :
For this, to English hearts, is holy ground.
The roar of London seems to beat on thee
Like waves from an advancing, rising sea
Beating upon a rock, whose noble form
Tells of the work of sunshine and of storm.
The Poetry of Worship in all Time,
The godward instinct of each age and clime,
Upon thy hallowed and historic wall
Is writ in characters majestical.

AT HAMPTON COURT.

PATHETIC in its bygone stateliness.
The Palace stands amidst its gardens fair.
The lawns are robed in summer's richest dress;
The fountains poise their rainbows in the air.
The river 'neath the terrace-balustrade,
Flows on its way, as silvery and serene,
As when King Charles lay dreaming in the shade,
Or Marlborough talked of Blenheim to the Queen.
But better than its actual memories
Is that sweet influence that in it lies :
For in its quaint old courts, and pleasant ways,
We meet the spirit of departed days.
The place is fine alike to heart and eye :—
By Nature blessed, and dowered by History.

APRIL DAYS.

No settled purpose holds these April days ;
But shine and shadow counterchange the hours :
March winds dispute the sun's advancing rays ;
And rainbows fleet across the fleeting show'rs.
The blurrs of winter chill the blossoming bow'rs,
And mock the blackbirds' bright antiphonies.
Shy buds expand, and trees burst forth in flow'rs,
Wooed by the sunshine's golden flatteries,
To face the anger of rebuking skies.
And thus it is, sweet youth, with all thy years,
Thy blossoming thoughts are washed by sudden tears ;
Thy sunniest hopes are fused with Wintry fears.
For Spring hath not the Summer's statelier calm :
And, having it, would lose its proper charm.

"GOOD IN EVERYTHING."

Dark pool, that slimes with moss the fallen tree,
And stagnates, thick with pulp and rotted weed,
Thou art not all unlovely: for in thee
The skies reflected lie.   Their blue, indeed,
Is stained by thine uncleanness: yet the light
Doth hide thy rank impurities from sight,
And paints them with its splendour.   Is the creed
That says in vilest things we still may find
A hint of what is beautiful and bright,
A vain one?   He, who with an earnest mind,
Wishes to find light, finds it everywhere!
In this dark pool some touch of glory lies.
It seems but filth: yet gaze with kindlier eyes,
And lo! a bit of heaven is shining there!

TO NATURE.

From streets and London life I gladly turn
To unfrequented fields, and homely ways;
Well pleased to sit at Nature's feet, and learn
The quiet lessons of sweet summer days.
The skies and seas, they will be kind and good;
And not refuse to give me brotherhood.
The hills and forests will not say me nay,
Nor shun to-morrow whom they love to-day.
Tired am I, and full of foolish fears:
My eyes are dulled with weak, but bitter tears.
So do I come, O Nature, to thy feet.
Ah! take me, Mother! calm and strengthen me:
That I, from life's mistakes and self-deceit,
May rest awhile, forgetting all but thee!

THE LOVER'S SECRET.

" YELLOW-HAIRED maiden, so busy a-gleaning,
   Why are you singing so blithely, I pray?
Have you discovered the spirit and meaning
   Of all that is glad in the long summer day?"

" Yea: I have found it : but not to reveal it.
   Need is there none I should give you the clue.
Nature, she taketh small pains to conceal it!
   Ah, good my lad, is it hidden from you?"

" If that it be, it is surely your mission
   Here to proclaim 'Lo, the path and the way!'
To say it will open to such a petition,
   And such is the tribute its votaries pay."

"''Tis born of no sweetness in opening flower ;
    'Tis sung by no nightingale under the tree :
Nor, rainbow-like, comes it of sunshine or shower ;
    Nor told of wild winds that sweep in from the sea."

" Lives it in valleys ? is't throned in the mountain ?
    Do stars up in heaven emblazon its name ?
Who knoweth its source ? or what eyes see its fountain ?
    And is it revealed in crystal or flame ?"

" It walketh the world in Sweetness and Beauty ;
    Its feet are with courage and purity shod :
Unselfishness robes it : 'tis crowned of Duty :
    And those who have seen it are conscious of God."

" I see it : I see it : though darkly and blindly !
    It speaks in your voice, and its music is strong :
It shines in your eyes, and its splendour is kindly :—
    The secret is mine :—I can join in your song."

AN IDLE DAY.

THE day is idle :—and idle am I !
   I care to do naught but lie and dream ;
As I gaze with half-closed eyes at the sky,
   And the diamond prisms that sparkle and beam
Over the top of the sand-hills high,
   Where the sails of the far-off vessels gleam.

Here could I lie all the happy day,
Content to dream the hours away !
Happy in knowing that you were by.
Whilst the wonder of open sea and sky,
And the sweet fresh scent of the ocean brine,
Revive my soul like bread and wine.
Our hearts are one with the sunlit scene ;
   With the sounds that fill the generous air ;
With the sea-weeds purple and brown and green ;
   With the delicate sand-flowers blooming there ;

With the pink and white shells that lie at our feet ;
With the sail-flecked horizon, hazy with heat ;
With the boats that swing in the purple bay ;
And the freedom of Nature who laughs whilst she may
In the God-given joy of the Summer Day.

So here let us lie on the yellow sea-sand,
　　Grasses, and shells and sea-weeds among.
We are monarchs of earth, and kings in the land,
　　Though no sceptre be given, no pæan be sung !
For we've sunshine and air :—we lie, hand in hand ;—
　　We hope, and remember :—we breathe, and are young !

A LESSON.

Lo! every year, on Autumn's chilling breeze,
   The Frost draws near to strip the branches clean :
But still the infinitely hopeful trees,
   The Winter gone, put on their robes of green.

Each year the miracle of Spring is wrought
   As freshly as in Eden's primal bowers :
And raw December's reign is set at naught
   By April's vernal rains, and May-time's flowers.

Hence let me learn from Disappointment's face
   To turn aside with undespairing heart :—
Ready to meet fresh Hope with fitting grace,
   And bear in any spring a timely part.

A NEW YEAR'S GREETING.

HERE by the open window,
  On this sweet New Year's Day,
I'm striving hard to listen
  To what Earth has to say.
The air is mild and quiet,
  The ground is dark and soft,
The flood-tides of the river
  Gleam in the willow-croft.
All things are calm and pensive :
  And from the fir-woods there
The twitter of the robin
  Makes sweet the sleepy air.
O twinkling shrubs and hollies,
  O ferns in sheltered nook,
O hoarse, full-throated warblings
  Of yonder rain-filled brook,
Ye have a voice, a language,
  An untranslated speech :

And all my heart is yearning
    To learn what you can teach.
My life is not a-tuneful
    To your majestic keys ;
My ears are all too fevered
    For your pure harmonies.
But, as I listen humbly,
    And try to understand,
A voice most sweet and solemn
    Comes up from off the land.
I cannot tell the message,
    Or what the voice I hear :—
It sings for all who listen—
    New songs for every ear !

TO MY BROTHER FRANK.

When the heather's regal purple
    Changes into dusty hue ;
And the morning brambles glisten,
    Filmed with webs asheen with dew :
When the bracken, brown and amber,
    Glorifies the forest's gloom ;
And the gossamers go sailing
    Over moors of heath and broom :
When the distance grows more dreamy,
    Soft with lines of golden haze ;
Whilst the scent of mellowing apples
    Fills the orchard's pleasant ways :
When the children go out nutting
    Through the wood, and down the lane ;
And the ricks are thatched and finished,
    And the garners stored with grain :
When the lingering flowers seem fairer

From the sense of Winter near ;
And regret for Summer faded
    Makes the sunshine doubly dear :
Then the memories re-awaken
    Of that sad and hallowed day
When your spirit, O my brother,
    Passed from us and earth away.

There was once a time, my brother,
    When you made the world to me ;
When I could not dream of gladness
    Separate from thoughts of thee.
To my childish hero-worship
    You were monarch in the land :
Everything was safe and hopeful
    When you held me by the hand.
Now the sense of separation
    Seldom stirs me to the heart :
And I wonder to remember
    How I thought we ne'er should part :
How I used to feel 'twere hopeless
    To conceive what life would be
If its sorrows, joys, and dangers
    Were not known and told to thee.

Ah, pathetic strange reversal !
    Sorrow's natural Nemesis !
Now 'twould seem as strange to see thee,
    As it once had seemed to miss !
Yet, although through dole or pleasure
    I may take my onward way,
Seeming but to feel the Present,
    And the friendships of To-day ;
This I know,—your loss is written
    Over all my manhood's years :
Writ on plans that miss fulfilment,
    Writ in Failure's bitter tears :
Writ in deep and strong conviction
    That the only path for me,
Which can lead me on or upward,
    Is the path marked out by thee.
Thus my life, beloved brother,
    Or in Failure or Success,
Mourns in this your loss and silence,
    Feels in that your love's impress :
And in all its deepest feelings,
    All its little sum of good,
Answers to the recollections
    Of our deathless brotherhood.

Ah ! the world is all too busy !
　　Present joys and present strife,
Drown, with Babel sound, the voices
　　That give dignity to life.
And amidst the press and hurry
　　Of these overcrowded times,
Nothing is so soon forgotten
　　As the sound of funeral chimes.
In some hearts, unseen by any,
　　Silent sorrow may abide ;
But the world compels our faces,
　　And puts memory aside.
Each hour brings its claim upon us,
　　Every day new faces throng,
All day long life's hurrying currents
　　Bear us ruthlessly along.
There seems little pause or leisure
　　To remember, or to think.
Recollection, contemplation,
　　These, with all their issues, sink
Out of sight amid the turmoil :—
　　So much poorer, we, of heart !
We are cumbered with much serving,
　　And we lose the better part.

Therefore I am glad September
    Comes each year my path across,
To recall the old affection,
    And remind me of my loss.
Therefore 'tis its pensive beauty
    Hath for me a voice divine,
Brings to me a special message,
    Comes with glory and a sign.
May the golden days of Autumn
    Always through the passing years
Re-create this sweet sad sorrow,
    And revive these hallowing tears.
Let them never cease to call me
    For a while from noise and strife,
To a silent contemplation
    Of his pure and blameless life :
Life he seemed to make heroic,
    Though a life shut in from praise,
Simply by the way he lived it,
    And the fashion of its days :
Of a path, which, spite of weakness,
    Bravely to the end he trod :
Of his calm belief in patience ;
    And his simple faith in God.

TO A FRIEND.

LIGHT and Peace be with you ever!
Clearness, strength, and high endeavour,
Will that works, and falters never,

  Lead you upward into Light!
Life may give to thee her treasures,
Flowers, and songs, and heaped-up pleasures,
Foaming cups and brimming measures,

  Hopes that sparkle in their flight:
Friends may cheer the way before thee;
Love may sing the old, old story:
Art display to thee her glory:

  Fair success her laurelled height:
May you then have strength in choosing;
Joy in seeing, and in using;
Joy that brings no after losing,

  Holds no subtle taint of blight.

But should sorrow come anear thee ;
And few friendly voices cheer thee ;
And your heart grow faint and weary
    At the daily fret and fight :
If thy Faith, by struggle broken,
Fail of any certain token
That a Master voice hath spoken,
    Or of what may be the Right :
May you then hold fast the powers
That you've owned, in calmest hours,
Seem to make this life of ours
    Most heroic and most bright.
Let no siren-voice uproot thee
From the faith that highest Beauty
Lies in doing simplest Duty
    Even in your own despite.
Views may change as life advances ;
Present faiths grow future fancies ;
Youthful hopes and young romances
    May grow faint, or vanish quite ;
But through all things transitory,
May some fair Ideal of glory,
Some high Purpose, shine before thee,
    Cloud by day, and fire by night :

Keep your faith to that unshaken :
And, whatever path be taken,
Be you followed or forsaken,

  On your life's page it will write
That New Name, mysterious, splendid,
That awaits, when life is ended,
Those whose knees are not found bended

  To things seen, or Mammon's might.
Now our paths seem bound for ever :
But, it may be, life's endeavour
Widely may our footsteps sever,

  'Mid the tumult of the fight :
But or whether near, or parted,
Still our love shall live, true-hearted.
In life's morning it was started

  May it last till it be night !

A MOMENT OF FAIRYLAND.

A COTTAGE, and its garden plot,
   Bosomed in deep, ambrosial wood :—
Flower and fruit, despising not
   A sweet unenvious brotherhood :—
A scent of currant-bush and box,
   Hot with the summer :—everywhere,
A blaze of blossom :—and bright flocks
   Of butterflies in sunlit air :—
A little fairyland it seemed !
   And Queen of all, by fairy lore,
A girl, where light thro' foliage gleamed.
   Sat singing by the cottage door.

The air was full of glittering wings,
   And all alive with pleasant sound ;
Leaf-shadows lay, in quivering rings,
   That danced and flickered on the ground :

The honeysuckles overhead
    Swayed in the draughts of scented air :
And foxglove spires, white and red,
    Grew either side the broken stair
That sloped to where the chestnuts made
    Their branches roof a mossy dell,
Where ferns were growing in the shade,
    And water dripped adown a well.

The maiden sang : happy and strong,
    The sweet young voice rose heavenward :—
It was a simple, homely song,
    But touched some true and perfect chord.
It seemed the poem of the place—
    At one with all the summer day !
It, and the maiden's upturned face,
    Answered the sunshine every way.
Once she looked round : I thought she saw
    My shadow as I passed along :—
But no ! she dreamed on, as before—
    The dream that floated on the song.

I felt myself some youthful prince,
    With plumed brow, and belted thigh :

A hundred fairy tales, long since
    Forgotten, flashed to memory.
Many a sylvan form and elf
    Peeped from rich bloom and leafy tree :
And Puck, and Ariel herself
    Came riding on a bumble-bee.
That was the Maiden of the Wood :—
    My boyhood's wonderland was found !
And as beneath those trees I stood,
    I felt it was enchanted ground !

I heard a voice within call loud ;
    The maiden rose and went inside :—
The light was shut off by a cloud :—
    The colour paled :—the sunlight died !
'Twas only for a moment's space,
    That I beheld that woodland dell,
And looked upon that Maiden's face ;
    But yet—though how, I cannot tell,- -
I touched on Fairyland that day,
    Just for one moment—am I wrong ?—
A flash !   It came, and passed away,
    Upon a smile, and in a song.

AT THE ALTAR-STEPS.

OUR life has been unfruitful, vain ;
    Not dedicate to Thee :—,
We have not laboured for Thy Reign :—
    Unworthy servants, we !

The first-fruits of our days were not
    Upon Thine altar placed :
But plucked, and thrown aside to rot
    In Youth's ungarnered waste.

And Thou hast seen us dancing round
    The golden calves of earth ;
Not staying for the thunder's sound
    Our thoughtless songs of mirth.

Yea : with great Sinai all aflame
    With judgments of the years,
We have but veiled our eyes with shame,
    And dulled with sin our ears.

And is it now too late, good Lord?
    Must we expect Thy frown?
And is there only now the sword,
    For us, who scorned the crown?

Ah! but Thy mercy it is great,
    Broad as the steadfast heaven:
It cannot ever be too late
    As long as hope is given.

Thy Name of Father we can trust;
    Trust what its meanings tell:
For like a line of light 'tis thrust
    Athwart the glooms of hell.

Our lips are ignorant of prayer;
    Our knees are stiff with pride:
But here—upon Thy lowest stair—
    We plead the Crucified.

Fumes rich and rank from Sin's hot night
    Are steaming round us still;
And many a phantom poison-light
    Still stars the realms of Ill;—

M

Still are we prone to blind our eyes,
    And grovel in the mud ;
And Will is lame to exorcise
    The devil in the blood.

We fall, and fall : but Thou art strong ;
    Thy Pity will not pause :—
And if Thou seest all the Wrong,
    Thou knowest all the Cause !

Oppressed, and torn a hundred ways ;
    Awed with life's mysteries ;
Blinded with straining eager gaze,
    Into unanswering skies ;

Ay,—spent with battling unseen Powers ;
    We turn us back at length
To That which wiser heads than ours
    Have found was Light and Strength.

So, like young children saying prayers
    Beside the mother's knee,
We kneel us at Thine altar-stairs,
    And lift our hands to Thee.

O, YET the birds in vale and wood are singing joyous
   trills ;
The rains refresh the meadow lawns; the sunshine
   warms the hills ;—

The sunset and the dawn still come to glorify the sky ;
The lilies by the waterside are blooming peacefully :—

The children going down the lane, sing out, and shout
   for glee ;
And nothing seems to miss the life that was the world
   to me.

High up, the twittering swallows skim the air with
   happy flight ;
Like crimson flames they flicker as they turn athwart
   the light.

The evening primrose wakes to keep its fairy vigil
    watch ;
Calmly the smoke goes up from hearths beneath the
    cottage thatch.

And pleasantly the river flows to meet the far-off sea :—
And nothing seems to miss the life that was the world
    to me.

AT DUSK.

Now let us own that, one by one,
The lights of life that round us shone,
In hopeful youth, about our heart,
Begin to darken and depart.

'Tis thus that oft the morning's gold
Dies into cloud-webs, dark and cold :
And rosy promises of day
Are lost in skies of level gray.

Sick Failure, come, and crown Success :—
Come Love, join hands with Selfishness :—
What colour is't that will not fade ?
What man too lofty to degrade ?

Age comes to mar youth's godlike grace :
It draws strange lines about the face :
Life dwindles into narrow ways ;
And silence cometh on apace.

And so we come to chiefly bless,
And seek for, sleep—forgetfulness :—
Forgetfulness of Life's mistake:
Of hearts worn all too tough to break :

Of proud, strong Youth : and Happiness :
Of what the world calls our Success :
And of the Memories that are known
To us—ah me !—to us alone.

LET us walk in, and have a word or two.
The Green-room :—ah ! you know it, sir, I see.
Once it was thronged by sprightly wits and beaux :
Or so, at least, the older actors say.
Now 'tis but seldom used : its day is past.
Last week 'twas given up to "properties :"
But it is tidy now.   Shall we sit down ?
You are a friend, sir, of the management.
I'm glad to know you.   We but seldom have
The honour of a visitor—of one,
At least, I care to see—behind the scenes.
No, I have time enough.   I am not on
In this Act or the next :—a tedious part
That opens famously, and makes its mark,

Then disappears, and is forgotten flat:
And then turns up again, just at the last,
And people ask, "Why, who on earth is this?
Oh yes, of course; that man in Act the first.
We had forgotten him." A part I hate.
Hard work, and small effects, with tedious waits.
Not tedious though to-night, and thanks to you.

But the part fits me, now I come to think.
Hard work, and small effects, with tedious waits!
Waits, sure enough, more than enough of them.
I've waited now for years, I think, for what?
Well, many things: perhaps to play King Lear,
George Barnwell, Romeo, or Doricourt:—
Perhaps to save enough, sir, to retire,
And hoe the cabbages and celery
In some suburban cottage,—happy end!
Perhaps—perhaps—who knows the foolish things
I may have waited for—ay, wait for still!
I scarcely know myself; and would not tell
Even to that long looking-glass (that's seen,
No doubt, so much of life! and which to-night
Would make believe that I am old and gray!
This is a wig, you see: I wear it thus:

My own hair at the sides here works in well,
And makes it very natural, does it not?)
Not even to that glass would I tell the things
I've waited for—so long that waiting is
The thing itself—for it, the thing is gone :
But still the waiting, in itself a hope,
Remains.   And that is something in a world
Where hopes, and salaries, are few, and small.

I jest, you see : a little.   Well, one must, I think.
We players are a merry race, they say.
" Merry and careless " is the character
That we are labelled with by other folks.
We wear the label, sir, most patiently.
" Hard work, with small effects, and tedious waits,"
Is sometimes written on the other side.
But that side we keep downwards, as is best,
Read only of each other and ourselves :
Save when a hand more kindly than most hands—
(More clever, say ; for many hands are kind.)
Lifts it, and reads : and then we take that hand,
And, being weak, hysterical perhaps,
By nature—merriment and carelessness
Turned inside out, you know—we press it—so.

To-morrow morning? Yes: at twelve o'clock.
You'll come and see me then: why, that is brave.
Ev'n as the dial verges nigh to noon
I shall await you at the outer gates.
Forgive the actor, sir, his trick of speech,
Caught from the melodramas of his youth.
I knew an actor once who always spoke
In grandiose, colloquial, mock blank-verse:
A merry fellow with a dismal face!
The expectation of a visitor
Is as unusual as the hour, alas!
The midnight twelve is oftener my time,
For entertainment: and the place—your ear!—
The parlour of the Swan.   Ah! you are shocked.
Not shocked!   And you will meet me there?   'Tis
        well.

Yes, I've played many parts, sir, in my time.
I've played a demon in a Pantomime:
A lovely thing, sir, to have done, you'll own.
I've ranged from Hamlet to A Voice Outside.
We'll have a laugh at many an episode
That I can tell you,—if you care to hear.

Born on the stage, sir, as the actors say.
My father was an actor.   As I lay,
Rocked in the cradle at my mother's feet,
The coverlet I slept so warm beneath
Was Lady Anne's black cotton velvet robe ;—
(Her favourite part.)—The earliest words I heard,
The "Gentle Jesus" of good Doctor Watts,—
" Now is the winter of our discontent,"—
And "absolutely for the last two nights."

A little dingy lodging in a street
That led from out an old cathedral close
Is my first recollection of a home.
But we were Arabs, and we pitched our tent
In many places.   In those days, you know,
There were the Circuits, as they called them then,
For the best theatres in the provinces.
My father and my mother well were known
Throughout the Norwich Circuit : and for years
They played in all the towns about, and dreamed
Of London as a dream too bright and high
For real fulfilment.   But they were content.
The scheme of theatres and professional life
Is changed : I speak of times quite passed away.

They had their little social circles then,
Nice, quiet, homely folk : and for their art,
I'm minded to believe they knew it, sir,
Far better than our actors know theirs now.
But let that pass.   The new school always smiles
Over the fond traditions of the old.
No one can quite decide—opinions all !
And I have mine : and so we'll let that pass.

My mother.   Ah, I still am but a child
At thought of her.   She was an angel, sir.
She entertained the world, not the world her.
The world was singularly unaware.
But women far less talented than she
Have made a name,—whilst she—ah, well, poor
      dear!—
Her name is on a few old play-bills still ;
(I have them in my box) and somewhere too
In that Great Book of Life where blameless lives
Are written, as she taught me at her knee.
I cannot speak about her very well.
Childhood still holds me when I think of her.
'Tis well, in such a life as mine has been
To have a corner where your manhood stops,

Drops down upon its stiffened knees awhile,
And says its "Gentle Jesus" like a child.
I talk too much.   Your kindness leads me on.
Keep we our linen and our wool apart.
Look at this girl : she plays our Chambermaids.
Pretty ?—a good girl, too.   "God ye good den,"
Your scene just coming on ?   There! you are "called."
You'll see Bill Turner in a private box
Upon the prompt side.   Ah ! he's come to see
The local talent, and to find a "star"
For his next Pantomime : so now's your chance !
Laugh out your best.   Her laugh, sir, is her forte.
You know this gentleman, my dear ?—ah, so !
There : laugh like that, and Turner offers you
Your twenty pounds a week.   Go in, and win.

A good girl :—did you notice how she laughed ?
A pretty laugh—a very pretty laugh !
It moves me deeply, for—I weary you !
No ?—well, I will talk.   I'm garrulous to-night.
What was I saying?   Oh, her laugh ;—ah, yes :
I said it moved me, did I ?   Yes : of course :
Such laughter moves us all, you know.
The dullest audience fain must answer it.

I did not mean that? how do you know that?
You read between the lines!—an actor born!
Go on the stage : you'd prosper well, I'm sure.
A very good stage face and figure too.
You'd make a perfect County Paris now;
Charles Surface, too.—We'll see you on the boards.
Rub once against the wings, you're booked!

                   Her laugh?
It moves me; yes.   For it reminds me, sir,
Of laughter I have heard.   A silvery laugh,
That laughed me first to happiness, then scorn!
The old, old story?   Yes, no doubt : though told,
As it is always told, as if the tale
Were heard then for the first and only time.
When will it tire of being told and heard?
Well, that would be the saddest day of all.
Come, old, old story; sung, or whispered low;
Given in laughter, or in silent gaze;
All ears are straining for you! even mine,
Dulled with the voices of my many years,
Under this wretched wig and feathered hat,
Still listen to your echoes; and confess
I would not lose them, though they hurt me so.

"Twas thirty years ago, at Christmas time :
Red Riding Hood : I was a youngster then,
Scarce twenty-two, and played the harlequin.
Can you be interested in the life,
The very human life and happiness,
Of this young harlequin ?   His limbs were strong
Beneath the spangles and the red and gold.
And all the passion of a heart that loves,
That loves, and hopes, and has its world to win,
Made the wild folly of the "comic scenes"
A drama that was beautiful to him.

"The short, but simple annals of the poor"
Doubtless read strangely to the rich and great.
The loves of harlequin and columbine
Are difficult to treat of seriously.
Were I elsewhere, or you—well, not yourself—
I should not try to do so.   But this room,
My wig and paint perhaps, that massive cup
Of gilder plaister, with its paper flowers,
Befit the tale : and, stranger still to say,
Give it a life and make it natural.

My mother did not act when things went well

With me—at least not since my father's death :
And that same Christmas things went very well.
For I was what they call "a useful man"
Upon the stage.   Old men, or youthful swains,
Comedy, Tragedy, Melodrama, Farce,
Ready for all and each was I, in turn.
A famous dancer, too.   And, as it chanced,
Just as the Pantomime was well rehearsed,
Our harlequin falls ill.   Catastrophe!
The management is in despair.   I go :
And, for a rise of salary, consent
To fill the gap.   And so, on Boxing night,
I leap with mask and bat upon the stage
A full-grown harlequin.   You see I speak
About myself : 'tis easier.   For, of Her
I find it hard to speak.   'Tis difficult
To tell a tale if different points of view
Are seen : some plainlier than your own.
Then I was blind to all save what I felt.
Now I can see, and, seeing, I grow dumb.
I was to blame.   Yet telling all the tale
'Twould   seem   the   telling   gave   some   sort   of
          blame
To her, although I blamed myself alone.

Think of us not in spangles and in gauze,
But in a cloth coat and a simple gown :
Yes, it was simple then, in those old days.
Ah ! we were happy ! and she laughed a laugh
That laughed away all reason and all thought.
My mother went upon the stage again.
The old black velvet robe of Lady Anne,—
Ah, God forgive me !—it was trimmed afresh.
She went from me.   She told me once for all,
Bravely and simply, what she thought and felt.
" I cannot stay.   No shame has ever touched
My home," she said, "in childhood, or as wife.
My father, mother, husband, all have walked
A difficult world with footsteps clean and firm.
My son, I hoped, would always follow theirs.
Till now, he has : but now—I cannot stay.
Yet ere I go I use the mother's right
To tell you what you do, and how you stand.
You love the girl :—Love has no choice, I know :—
Marry her, and your love may make her true.
'Twere best I should not stay, were she your wife :
'Twere worse than worst to stay as things are
        now.
You are a man—and you must choose your path."

N

I did.   No man lets any hand divide
His love and him, if he be truly man.
She went.   The hand that all my life I'd held,
Upheld by it at first, upholding next,
Was loosed from mine—and so I went my way.
But, sir, they met again one day, those hands.
When I was—left alone, she came to me.
I lay unconscious, stricken nigh to death.
We never partèd more.   She had no word
Of blame or anger then.   She understood.
An angel, as the phrase goes—nothing less!

When I was left alone, I said : ah, yes ;—
It came to that, of course, it came to that :—
Foregone conclusions, sir : a tale oft told!
Two years of happiness, of love, of joy!
I give the memory its due.   'Tis bright.
Even the bitter memory is sweet.
Joy passed is oft forgotten or ignored ;
And if it brought the candle and the sheet,
Is sometimes charged with never having been !
I do not so.   The joy was full and sweet.
Those two years are the centre of my life.
The bond between us riveted itself

With ties of time as well as those of love :
When all was snapped and broken like a thread.

How did it come about ?
                     Why, thus : the hope
That really lay the nearest to her heart
Was hope of fame, and rising in her art.
Oh, she was clever on the stage, that's sure.
At last—after those two short happy years—
A man of influence, we'll name no names,
Saw her one night.   I heard about it all
Long afterwards.   The offer came to her.
A London theatre and the leading parts.
An offer that might dazzle any one.
The thing she'd always dreamed of : here it was !
And with but one condition :—that not hard,
How could it be ?—to leave me.   And she went.
The silvery laughter died from out my life.

Once only have I heard it since.   Four years
Had passed, and Time had done its usual work :—
Is it beneficent or terrible ?
Time's smiles are always somewhat sinister :—
My life had reached a level once again.

She came down with a London company.
A few of us stock actors were kept on
As "understudies."   When the morning came—
'Twas Monday—they arrived on Sunday night—
My mother urged me not to go : she feared
I know not what.   I told her not to fear.
I went.   They were rehearsing : and I stood
Deep in the shadow.   She was on the stage.
She knew that I was in the company;
But she had grown a skilful actress now
Both on and off the stage.   She looked about,
And saw me standing in the shadow there.
No recognition moved her smiling face.
The laughter rippled on.   The place was dark.
And, going out, I stumbled on a trap,
And fell :—a foolish little accident
Which brought them kindly round me in a crowd.
Not hurt ?—How fortunate !—a nasty fall !—
And did I think that it was Boxing night,
I harlequin ? the low comedian asked.
They laughed it off.   She laughed.   I listened hard,
And thought—or was it that I liked to think ?—
It did not ring quite true to life that time.
The prompter told me some time afterwards

She asked if I was cast to act with her,
And when told, " no," he thought that she was glad.
The fellow, meaning kindly, I am sure,
Tried hard to tell me more of what she asked,
Etcetera—etcetera—but I,
I changed the subject.   Let us change it now.

You'll find my den a very curious place.
I gave you the address.   A narrow street :
A forge exactly opposite the house :
A great place all ablaze with furnaces :
Dante's Inferno in a modern street.
Sometimes, on short dark days, the crimson light
Stencils the window all across the room,
And on the ceiling—quite a weird effect.
My mother ?—no, sir : died ten years ago.
I miss her sorely, even to this day.
No one at home to keep the supper warm,
Or give the welcoming word that makes a home.
'Twere better for me were she living still ;
But not for her,—I'm very sure of that.
The Swan sees me too often now.   But then
What matters ? twelve o'clock must come !
Ring down the curtain, and go home to bed.

And if the home be—well !—what's the address ?—
You have it on the card :—why, on the way,
A glass, a smoke, a little friendly chat
Is pleasant.   You will find me at the Swan.

The act is ended.   Hark ! a double call !
I'm glad, sir, for the honour of the house.
A London manager is here to-night :
And that girl ought to make herself a name.
Another act to wait ! a tedious part.
I score, though, at the last—a splendid scene !
Folks have forgotten all about me clean :
The lady thinks I'm dead, and all's condoned ;
And then, when everything is going well,
I enter : Tableau ! a fine scene—immense !
But things don't happen so in life, I fear.

Good-night, and thank you.   I have talked too much.
Blame your own kindness : and, if you forgive,
At twelve, to-morrow, come to me.   To-night,
In this queer, gas-lit room, and in this dress,
False hair, and paint, and armour made of tin,
I've babbled of realities of life :
To-morrow, in my habit as I live,

With the blast-furnace lighting up the room.
I'll tell you of my mimic life, the stage.
I shall expect you.   Now I must be off
To make myself grown old by twenty years.
The process is soon done.   I know it well.
You go in front?   Give me a friendly hand.

THE END.

Printed by R & R. CLARK *Edinburgh.*

A LIST OF

KEGAN PAUL, TRENCH & CO.'S
PUBLICATIONS.

8. 86

1, *Paternoster Square,*
London.

A LIST OF

KEGAN PAUL, TRENCH & CO.'S

PUBLICATIONS.

CONTENTS.

GENERAL LITERATURE.

A. K. H. B.—From a Quiet Place. A Volume of Sermons. Crown 8vo, 5s.

ALEXANDER, William, D.D., Bishop of Derry.—The Great Question, and other Sermons. Crown 8vo, 6s.

ALLEN, Rev. R., M.A.—Abraham: his Life, Times, and Travels, 3800 years ago. Second Edition. Post 8vo, 6s.

ALLIES, T. W., M.A.—Per Crucem ad Lucem. The Result of a Life. 2 vols. Demy 8vo, 25s.

A Life's Decision. Crown 8vo, 7s. 6d.

AMHERST, Rev. W. J.—The History of Catholic Emancipation and the Progress of the Catholic Church in the British Isles (chiefly in England) from 1771-1820. 2 vols. Demy 8vo, 24s.

AMOS, Professor Sheldon.—The History and Principles of the Civil Law of Rome. An aid to the Study of Scientific and Comparative Jurisprudence. Demy 8vo. 16s.

Ancient and Modern Britons. A Retrospect. 2 vols. Demy 8vo, 24s.

ANDERDON, Rev. W. H.—Evenings with the Saints. Crown 8vo, 5s.

ANDERSON, David.—"Scenes" in the Commons. Crown 8vo, 5s.

ARISTOTLE.—The Nicomachean Ethics of Aristotle. Translated by F. H. Peters, M.A. Second Edition. Crown 8vo, 6s.

ARMSTRONG, Richard A., B.A.—Latter-Day Teachers. Six Lectures. Small crown 8vo, 2s. 6d.

AUBERTIN, J. J.—A Flight to Mexico. With Seven full-page Illustrations and a Railway Map of Mexico. Crown 8vo, 7s. 6d.

Six Months in Cape Colony and Natal. With Illustrations and Map. Crown 8vo, 6s.

BADGER, George Percy, D.C.L.—An English-Arabic Lexicon. In which the equivalent for English Words and Idiomatic Sentences are rendered into literary and colloquial Arabic. Royal 4to, 80s.

BAGEHOT, Walter.—The English Constitution. New and Revised Edition. Crown 8vo, 7s. 6d.

Lombard Street. A Description of the Money Market. Eighth Edition. Crown 8vo, 7s. 6d.

Essays on Parliamentary Reform. Crown 8vo, 5s.

Some Articles on the Depreciation of Silver, and Topics connected with it. Demy 8vo, 5s.

BAGOT, Alan, C.E.—Accidents in Mines: their Causes and Prevention. Crown 8vo, 6s.

The Principles of Colliery Ventilation. Second Edition, greatly enlarged. Crown 8vo, 5s.

The Principles of Civil Engineering as applied to Agriculture and Estate Management. Crown 8vo, 7s. 6d.

BAKER, Sir Sherston, Bart.—The Laws relating to Quarantine. Crown 8vo, 12s. 6d.

BAKER, Thomas.—A Battling Life; chiefly in the Civil Service. An Autobiography, with Fugitive Papers on Subjects of Public Importance. Crown 8vo, 7s. 6d.

BALDWIN, Capt. J. H.—The Large and Small Game of Bengal and the North-Western Provinces of India. With 20 Illustrations. New and Cheaper Edition. Small 4to, 10s. 6d.

BALLIN, Ada S. and F. L.—A Hebrew Grammar. With Exercises selected from the Bible. Crown 8vo, 7s. 6d.

BARCLAY, Edgar.—Mountain Life in Algeria. With numerous Illustrations by Photogravure. Crown 4to, 16s.

BARLOW, James W.—The Ultimatum of Pessimism. An Ethical Study. Demy 8vo, 6s.

Short History of the Normans in South Europe. Demy 8vo, 7s. 6d.

BAUR, *Ferdinand, Dr. Ph.*—A Philological Introduction to Greek and Latin for Students. Translated and adapted from the German, by C. KEGAN PAUL, M.A., and E. D. STONE, M.A. Third Edition. Crown 8vo, 6s.

BAYLY, *Capt. George.*—Sea Life Sixty Years Ago. A Record of Adventures which led up to the Discovery of the Relics of the long-missing Expedition commanded by the Comte de la Perouse. Crown 8vo, 3s. 6d.

BELLASIS, *Edward.*—The Money Jar of Plautus at the Oratory School. An Account of the Recent Representation. With Appendix and 16 Illustrations. Small 4to, sewed, 2s.

The New Terence at Edgbaston. Being Notices of the Performances in 1880 and 1881. With Preface, Notes, and Appendix. Third Issue. Small 4to, 1s. 6d.

BENN, *Alfred W.*—The Greek Philosophers. 2 vols. Demy 8vo, 28s.

Bible Folk-Lore. A Study in Comparative Mythology. Crown 8vo, 10s. 6d.

BIRD, *Charles, F.G.S.*—Higher Education in Germany and England. Being a brief Practical Account of the Organization and Curriculum of the German Higher Schools. With critical Remarks and Suggestions with reference to those of England. Small crown 8vo, 2s. 6d.

BLECKLY, *Henry.*—Socrates and the Athenians: An Apology. Crown 8vo, 2s. 6d.

BLOOMFIELD, *The Lady.*—Reminiscences of Court and Diplomatic Life. New and Cheaper Edition. With Frontispiece. Crown 8vo, 6s.

BLUNT, *The Ven. Archdeacon.*—The Divine Patriot, and other Sermons. Preached in Scarborough and in Cannes. New and Cheaper Edition. Crown 8vo, 4s. 6d.

BLUNT, *Wilfrid S.*—The Future of Islam. Crown 8vo, 6s.

Ideas about India. Crown 8vo. Cloth, 6s.

BODDY, *Alexander A.*—To Kairwân the Holy. Scenes in Muhammedan Africa. With Route Map, and Eight Illustrations by A. F. JACASSEY. Crown 8vo, 6s.

BOSANQUET, *Bernard.*—Knowledge and Reality. A Criticism of Mr. F. H. Bradley's "Principles of Logic." Crown 8vo, 9s.

BOUVERIE-PUSEY, *S. E. B.*—Permanence and Evolution. An Inquiry into the Supposed Mutability of Animal Types. Crown 8vo, 5s.

BOWEN, *H. C., M.A.*—Studies in English. For the use of Modern Schools. Eighth Thousand. Small crown 8vo, 1s. 6d.

English Grammar for Beginners. Fcap. 8vo, 1s.

Simple English Poems. English Literature for Junior Classes. In four parts. Parts I., II., and III., 6d. each. Part IV., 1s. Complete, 3s.

BRADLEY, F. H.—The Principles of Logic. Demy 8vo, 16s.

BRIDGETT, Rev. T. E.—History of the Holy Eucharist in Great Britain. 2 vols. Demy 8vo, 18s.

BROOKE, Rev. S. A.—Life and Letters of the Late Rev. F. W. Robertson, M.A. Edited by.

    I. Uniform with Robertson's Sermons. 2 vols. With Steel Portrait. 7s. 6d.
    II. Library Edition. With Portrait. 8vo, 12s.
    III. A Popular Edition. In 1 vol., 8vo, 6s.

The Fight of Faith. Sermons preached on various occasions. Fifth Edition. Crown 8vo, 7s. 6d.

The Spirit of the Christian Life. Third Edition. Crown 8vo, 5s.

Theology in the English Poets.- Cowper, Coleridge, Wordsworth, and Burns. Fifth Edition. Post 8vo, 5s.

Christ in Modern Life. Sixteenth Edition. Crown 8vo, 5s.

Sermons. First Series. Thirteenth Edition. Crown 8vo, 5s.

Sermons. Second Series. Sixth Edition. Crown 8vo, 5s.

BROWN, Rev. J. Baldwin, B.A.—The Higher Life. Its Reality, Experience, and Destiny. Sixth Edition. Crown 8vo, 5s.

Doctrine of Annihilation in the Light of the Gospel of Love. Five Discourses. Fourth Edition. Crown 8vo, 2s. 6d.

The Christian Policy of Life. A Book for Young Men of Business. Third Edition. Crown 8vo, 3s. 6d.

BROWN, Horatio F.—Life on the Lagoons. With two Illustrations and Map. Crown 8vo, 6s.

BROWNE, H. L.—Reason and Religious Belief. Crown 8vo, 3s. 6d.

BURDETT, Henry C.—Help in Sickness—Where to Go and What to Do. Crown 8vo, 1s. 6d.

Helps to Health. The Habitation—The Nursery—The Schoolroom and—The Person. With a Chapter on Pleasure and Health Resorts. Crown 8vo, 1s. 6d.

BURKE, The Late Very Rev. T. N.—His Life. By W. J. FITZPATRICK. 2 vols. With Portrait. Demy 8vo, 30s.

BURTON, Mrs. Richard.—The Inner Life of Syria, Palestine, and the Holy Land. Post 8vo, 6s.

CAPES, J. M.—The Church of the Apostles: an Historical Inquiry. Demy 8vo, 9s.

Carlyle and the Open Secret of His Life. By HENRY LARKIN. Demy 8vo, 14s.

CARPENTER, W. B., LL.D., M.D., F.R.S., etc.—The Principles of Mental Physiology. With their Applications to the Training and Discipline of the Mind, and the Study of its Morbid Conditions. Illustrated. Sixth Edition. 8vo, 12s.

Catholic Dictionary. Containing some Account of the Doctrine, Discipline, Rites, Ceremonies, Councils, and Religious Orders of the Catholic Church. By WILLIAM E. ADDIS and THOMAS ARNOLD, M.A. Third Edition. Demy 8vo, 21s.

CHEYNE, Rev. T. K.—The Prophecies of Isaiah. Translated with Critical Notes and Dissertations. 2 vols. Third Edition. Demy 8vo, 25s.

Circulating Capital. Being an Inquiry into the Fundamental Laws of Money. An Essay by an East India Merchant. Small crown 8vo, 6s.

CLAIRAUT.—Elements of Geometry. Translated by Dr. KAINES. With 145 Figures. Crown 8vo, 4s. 6d.

CLAPPERTON, Jane Hume.—Scientific Meliorism and the Evolution of Happiness. Large crown 8vo, 8s. 6d.

CLARKE, Rev. Henry James, A.K.C.—The Fundamental Science. Demy 8vo, 10s. 6d.

CLAYDEN, P. W.—Samuel Sharpe. Egyptologist and Translator of the Bible. Crown 8vo, 6s.

CLIFFORD, Samuel.—What Think Ye of the Christ? Crown 8vo, 6s.

CLODD, Edward, F.R.A.S.—The Childhood of the World: a Simple Account of Man in Early Times. Seventh Edition. Crown 8vo, 3s.
    A Special Edition for Schools. 1s.

    The Childhood of Religions. Including a Simple Account of the Birth and Growth of Myths and Legends. Eighth Thousand. Crown 8vo, 5s.
    A Special Edition for Schools. 1s. 6d.

    Jesus of Nazareth. With a brief sketch of Jewish History to the Time of His Birth. Small crown 8vo, 6s.

COGHLAN, J. Cole, D.D.—The Modern Pharisee and other Sermons. Edited by the Very Rev. H. H. DICKINSON, D.D., Dean of Chapel Royal, Dublin. New and Cheaper Edition. Crown 8vo, 7s. 6d.

COLE, George R. Fitz-Roy.—The Peruvians at Home. Crown 8vo, 6s.

COLERIDGE, Sara.—Memoir and Letters of Sara Coleridge. Edited by her Daughter. With Index. Cheap Edition. With Portrait. 7s. 6d.

Collects Exemplified. Being Illustrations from the Old and New Testaments of the Collects for the Sundays after Trinity. By the Author of "A Commentary on the Epistles and Gospels." Edited by the Rev. JOSEPH JACKSON. Crown 8vo, 5s.

CONNELL, A. K.—Discontent and Danger in India. Small crown 8vo, 3s. 6d.

The Economic Revolution of India. Crown 8vo, 4s. 6d.

COOK, Keningale, LL.D.—The Fathers of Jesus. A Study of the Lineage of the Christian Doctrine and Traditions. 2 vols. Demy 8vo, 28s.

CORY, William.—A Guide to Modern English History. Part I.—MDCCCXV.-MDCCCXXX. Demy 8vo, 9s. Part II.—MDCCCXXX.-MDCCCXXXV., 15s.

COTTERILL, H. B.—An Introduction to the Study of Poetry. Crown 8vo, 7s. 6d.

COTTON, H. J. S.—New India, or India in Transition. Third Edition. Crown 8vo, 4s. 6d.

COUTTS, Francis Burdett Money.—The Training of the Instinct of Love. With a Preface by the Rev. EDWARD THRING, M.A. Small crown 8vo, 2s. 6d.

COX, Rev. Sir George W., M.A., Bart.—The Mythology of the Aryan Nations. New Edition. Demy 8vo, 16s.

Tales of Ancient Greece. New Edition. Small crown 8vo, 6s.

A Manual of Mythology in the form of Question and Answer. New Edition. Fcap. 8vo, 3s.

An Introduction to the Science of Comparative Mythology and Folk-Lore. Second Edition. Crown 8vo, 7s. 6d.

COX, Rev. Sir G. W., M. A., Bart., and JONES, Eustace Hinton.—Popular Romances of the Middle Ages. Third Edition, in 1 vol. Crown 8vo, 6s.

COX, Rev. Samuel, D.D.—A Commentary on the Book of Job. With a Translation. Second Edition. Demy 8vo, 15s.

Salvator Mundi; or, Is Christ the Saviour of all Men? Tenth Edition. Crown 8vo, 5s.

The Larger Hope. A Sequel to "Salvator Mundi." Second Edition. 16mo, 1s.

The Genesis of Evil, and other Sermons, mainly expository. Third Edition. Crown 8vo, 6s.

Balaam. An Exposition and a Study. Crown 8vo, 5s.

Miracles. An Argument and a Challenge. Crown 8vo, 2s. 6d.

CRAVEN, Mrs.—A Year's Meditations. Crown 8vo, 6s.

CRAWFURD, Oswald.—**Portugal, Old and New.** With Illustrations and Maps. New and Cheaper Edition. Crown 8vo, 6s.

CROZIER, John Beattie, M.B.—**The Religion of the Future.** Crown 8vo, 6s.

CUNNINGHAM, W., B.D.—**Politics and Economics :** An Essay on the Nature of the Principles of Political Economy, together with a survey of Recent Legislation. Crown 8vo, 5s.

DANIELL, Clarmont.—**The Gold Treasure of India.** An Inquiry into its Amount, the Cause of its Accumulation, and the Proper Means of using it as Money. Crown 8vo, 5s.

Discarded Silver : a Plan for its Use as Money. Small crown, 8vo, 2s.

DANIEL, Gerard. **Mary Stuart : a Sketch and a Defence.** Crown 8vo, 5s.

DAVIDSON, Rev. Samuel, D.D., LL.D.—**Canon of the Bible :** Its Formation, History, and Fluctuations. Third and Revised Edition. Small crown 8vo, 5s.

The Doctrine of Last Things contained in the New Testament compared with the Notions of the Jews and the Statements of Church Creeds. Small crown 8vo, 3s. 6d.

DAWSON, Geo., M.A. **Prayers, with a Discourse on Prayer.** Edited by his Wife. First Series. Ninth Edition. Crown 8vo, 3s. 6d.

Prayers, with a Discourse on Prayer. Edited by GEORGE ST. CLAIR. Second Series. Crown 8vo, 6s.

Sermons on Disputed Points and Special Occasions. Edited by his Wife. Fourth Edition. Crown 8vo, 6s.

Sermons on Daily Life and Duty. Edited by his Wife. Fourth Edition. Crown 8vo, 6s.

The Authentic Gospel, and other Sermons. Edited by GEORGE ST. CLAIR, F.G.S. Third Edition. Crown 8vo, 6s.

Biographical Lectures. Edited by GEORGE ST. CLAIR, F.G.S. Large crown, 8vo, 7s. 6d.

DE JONCOURT, Madame Marie.—**Wholesome Cookery.** Third Edition. Crown 8vo, 3s. 6d.

Democracy in the Old World and the New. By the Author of "The Suez Canal, the Eastern Question, and Abyssinia," etc. Small crown 8vo, 2s. 6d.

DENT, H. C.—**A Year in Brazil.** With Notes on Religion, Meteorology, Natural History, etc. Maps and Illustrations. Demy 8vo, 18s.

Discourse on the Shedding of Blood, and The Laws of War. Demy 8vo, 2s. 6d.

DOUGLAS, Rev. Herman.—Into the Deep ; or, The Wonders of the Lord's Person. Crown 8vo, 2s. 6d.

DOWDEN, Edward, LL.D.—Shakspere : a Critical Study of his Mind and Art. Eighth Edition. Post 8vo, 12s.

Studies in Literature, 1789-1877. Third Edition. Large post 8vo, 6s.

Dulce Domum. Fcap. 8vo, 5s.

DU MONCEL, Count.—The Telephone, the Microphone, and the Phonograph. With 74 Illustrations. Third Edition. Small crown 8vo, 5s.

DURUY, Victor.—History of Rome and the Roman People. Edited by Prof. MAHAFFY. With nearly 3000 Illustrations. 4to. 6 vols. in 12 parts, 30s. each vol.

EDGEWORTH, F. Y.—Mathematical Psychics. An Essay on the Application of Mathematics to Social Science. Demy 8vo, 7s. 6d.

Educational Code of the Prussian Nation, in its Present Form. In accordance with the Decisions of the Common Provincial Law, and with those of Recent Legislation. Crown 8vo, 2s. 6d.

Education Library. Edited by PHILIP MAGNUS :—

An Introduction to the History of Educational Theories. By OSCAR BROWNING, M.A. Second Edition. 3s. 6d.

Old Greek Education. By the Rev. Prof. MAHAFFY, M.A. Second Edition. 3s. 6d.

School Management. Including a general view of the work of Education, Organization and Discipline. By JOSEPH LANDON. Fifth Edition. 6s.

EDWARDES, Major-General Sir Herbert B.—Memorials of his Life and Letters. By his Wife. With Portrait and Illustrations. 2 vols. Demy 8vo. 36s.

ELSDALE, Henry.—Studies in Tennyson's Idylls. Crown 8vo, 5s.

Emerson's (Ralph Waldo) Life. By OLIVER WENDELL HOLMES. English Copyright Edition. With Portrait. Crown 8vo, 6s.

Enoch the Prophet. The Book of. Archbishop LAURENCE'S Translation, with an Introduction by the Author of "The Evolution of Christianity." Crown 8vo, 5s.

Eranus. A Collection of Exercises in the Alcaic and Sapphic Metres. Edited by F. W. CORNISH, Assistant Master at Eton. Second Edition. Crown 8vo, 2s.

EVANS, Mark.—The Story of Our Father's Love, told to Children. Sixth and Cheaper Edition. With Four Illustrations. Fcap. 8vo, 1s. 6d.

"Fan Kwae" at Canton before Treaty Days 1825–1844. By an old Resident. With Frontispiece. Crown 8vo, 5s.

Faith of the Unlearned, The. Authority, apart from the Sanction of Reason, an Insufficient Basis for It. By "One Unlearned." Crown 8vo, 6s.

FEIS, Jacob.—Shakspere and Montaigne. An Endeavour to Explain the Tendency of Hamlet from Allusions in Contemporary Works. Crown 8vo, 5s.

FLOREDICE, W. H.—A Month among the Mere Irish. Small crown 8vo. Second Edition. 3s. 6d.

Frank Leward. Edited by CHARLES BAMPTON. Crown 8vo, 7s. 6d.

FULLER, Rev. Morris.—The Lord's Day ; or, Christian Sunday. Its Unity, History, Philosophy, and Perpetual Obligation. Sermons. Demy 8vo, 10s. 6d.

GARDINER, Samuel R., and J. BASS MULLINGER, M.A.— Introduction to the Study of English History. Second Edition. Large crown 8vo, 9s.

GARDNER, Dorsey.—Quatre Bras, Ligny, and Waterloo. A Narrative of the Campaign in Belgium, 1815. With Maps and Plans. Demy 8vo, 16s.

GELDART, E. M.—Echoes of Truth. Sermons, with a Short Selection of Prayers and an Introductory Sketch, by the Rev. C. B. UPTON. Crown 8vo, 6s.

Genesis in Advance of Present Science. A Critical Investigation of Chapters I.–IX. By a Septuagenarian Beneficed Presbyter. Demy 8vo. 10s. 6d.

GEORGE, Henry.—Progress and Poverty : An Inquiry into the Causes of Industrial Depressions, and of Increase of Want with Increase of Wealth. The Remedy. Fifth Library Edition. Post 8vo, 7s. 6d. Cabinet Edition. Crown 8vo, 2s. 6d. Also a Cheap Edition. Limp cloth, 1s. 6d. Paper covers, 1s.

> **Protection, or Free Trade.** An Examination of the Tariff Question, with especial regard to the Interests of Labour. Crown 8vo, 5s.

> **Social Problems.** Fourth Thousand. Crown 8vo, 5s. Cheap Edition. Paper covers, 1s.

GLANVILL, Joseph.—Scepsis Scientifica ; or, Confest Ignorance, the Way to Science ; in an Essay of the Vanity of Dogmatizing and Confident Opinion. Edited, with Introductory Essay, by JOHN OWEN. Elzevir 8vo, printed on hand-made paper, 6s.

Glossary of Terms and Phrases. Edited by the Rev. H. PERCY SMITH and others. Second and Cheaper Edition. Medium 8vo, 7s. 6d.

GLOVER, F., M.A.—Exempla Latina. A First Construing Book, with Short Notes, Lexicon, and an Introduction to the Analysis of Sentences. Second Edition. Fcap. 8vo, 2s.

GOLDSMID, Sir Francis Henry, Bart., Q.C., M.P.—Memoir of. With Portrait. Second Edition, Revised. Crown 8vo, 6s.

GOODENOUGH, Commodore J. G.—Memoir of, with Extracts from his Letters and Journals. Edited by his Widow. With Steel Engraved Portrait. Third Edition. Crown 8vo, 5s.

GORDON, Major-Genl. C. G.—His Journals at Kartoum. Printed from the original MS. With Introduction and Notes by A. EGMONT HAKE. Portrait, 2 Maps, and 30 Illustrations. Two vols., demy 8vo, 21s. Also a Cheap Edition in 1 vol., 6s.

Gordon's (General) Last Journal. A Facsimile of the last Journal received in England from GENERAL GORDON. Reproduced by Photo-lithography. Imperial 4to, £3 3s.

Events in his Life. From the Day of his Birth to the Day of his Death. By Sir H. W. GORDON. With Maps and Illustrations. Demy 8vo, 18s.

GOSSE, Edmund.—Seventeenth Century Studies. A Contribution to the History of English Poetry. Demy 8vo, 10s. 6d.

GOULD, Rev. S. Baring, M.A.—Germany, Present and Past. New and Cheaper Edition. Large crown 8vo, 7s. 6d.

GOWAN, Major Walter E.—A. Ivanoff's Russian Grammar. (16th Edition.) Translated, enlarged, and arranged for use of Students of the Russian Language. Demy 8vo, 6s.

GOWER, Lord Ronald. My Reminiscences. MINIATURE EDITION, printed on hand-made paper, limp parchment antique, 10s. 6d.

Last Days of Mary Antoinette. An Historical Sketch. With Portrait and Facsimiles. Fcap. 4to, 10s. 6d.

Notes of a Tour from Brindisi to Yokohama, 1883–1884. Fcap. 8vo, 2s. 6d.

GRAHAM, William, M.A.—The Creed of Science, Religious, Moral, and Social. Second Edition, Revised. Crown 8vo, 6s.

The Social Problem, in its Economic, Moral, and Political Aspects. Demy 8vo, 14s.

GREY, Rowland.—In Sunny Switzerland. A Tale of Six Weeks. Second Edition. Small crown 8vo, 5s.

Lindenblumen and other Stories. Small crown 8vo, 5s.

GRIMLEY, Rev. H. N., M.A.—Tremadoc Sermons, chiefly on the Spiritual Body, the Unseen World, and the Divine Humanity. Fourth Edition. Crown 8vo, 6s.

GUSTAFSON, Alex.—The Foundation of Death. Third Edition. Crown 8vo, 5s.

GUSTAFSON, Alex.—continued.

Some Thoughts on Moderation. Reprinted from a Paper read at the Reeve Mission Room, Manchester Square, June 8, 1885. Crown 8vo, 1s.

*HADDON, Caroline.—*The Larger Life, Studies in Hinton's Ethics. Crown 8vo, 5s.

*HAECKEL, Prof. Ernst.—*The History of Creation. Translation revised by Professor E. RAY LANKESTER, M.A., F.R.S. With Coloured Plates and Genealogical Trees of the various groups of both Plants and Animals. 2 vols. Third Edition. Post 8vo, 32s.

The History of the Evolution of Man. With numerous Illustrations. 2 vols. Post 8vo, 32s.

A Visit to Ceylon. Post 8vo, 7s. 6d.

Freedom in Science and Teaching. With a Prefatory Note by T. H. HUXLEY, F.R.S. Crown 8vo, 5s.

HALF-CROWN SERIES :—

A Lost Love. By ANNA C. OGLE [Ashford Owen].

Sister Dora : a Biography. By MARGARET LONSDALE.

True Words for Brave Men : a Book for Soldiers and Sailors. By the late CHARLES KINGSLEY.

Notes of Travel : being Extracts from the Journals of Count VON MOLTKE.

English Sonnets. Collected and Arranged by J. DENNIS.

Home Songs for Quiet Hours. By the Rev. Canon R. H. BAYNES.

Hamilton, Memoirs of Arthur, B.A., of Trinity College, Cambridge. Crown 8vo, 6s.

*HARRIS, William.—*The History of the Radical Party in Parliament. Demy 8vo, 15s.

*HARROP, Robert.—*Bolingbroke. A Political Study and Criticism. Demy 8vo, 14s.

*HART, Rev. J. W. T.—*The Autobiography of Judas Iscariot. A Character Study. Crown 8vo, 3s. 6d.

*HAWEIS, Rev. H. R., M.A.—*Current Coin. Materialism—The Devil—Crime—Drunkenness—Pauperism—Emotion—Recreation—The Sabbath. Fifth Edition. Crown 8vo, 5s.

Arrows in the Air. Fifth Edition. Crown 8vo, 5s.

Speech in Season. Fifth Edition. Crown 8vo, 5s.

Thoughts for the Times. Thirteenth Edition. Crown 8vo, 5s.

Unsectarian Family Prayers. New Edition. Fcap. 8vo, 1s. 6d.

HAWKINS, Edwards Comerford.—**Spirit and Form.** Sermons preached in the Parish Church of Leatherhead. Crown 8vo, 6s.

HAWTHORNE, Nathaniel.—**Works.** Complete in Twelve Volumes. Large post 8vo, 7s. 6d. each volume.

> VOL. I. TWICE-TOLD TALES.
>   II. MOSSES FROM AN OLD MANSE.
>   III. THE HOUSE OF THE SEVEN GABLES, AND THE SNOW IMAGE.
>   IV. THE WONDERBOOK, TANGLEWOOD TALES, AND GRAND-FATHER'S CHAIR.
>   V. THE SCARLET LETTER, AND THE BLITHEDALE ROMANCE.
>   VI. THE MARBLE FAUN. [Transformation.]
> VII. VIII. } OUR OLD HOME, AND ENGLISH NOTE-BOOKS.
>   IX. AMERICAN NOTE-BOOKS.
>   X. FRENCH AND ITALIAN NOTE-BOOKS.
>   XI. SEPTIMIUS FELTON, THE DOLLIVER ROMANCE, FANSHAWE, AND, IN AN APPENDIX, THE ANCESTRAL FOOTSTEP.
>   XII. TALES AND ESSAYS, AND OTHER PAPERS, WITH A BIO-GRAPHICAL SKETCH OF HAWTHORNE.

HEATH, Francis George.—**Autumnal Leaves.** Third and cheaper Edition. Large crown 8vo, 6s.

Sylvan Winter. With 70 Illustrations. Large crown 8vo, 14s.

HENNESSY, Sir John Pope.—**Ralegh in Ireland.** With his Letters on Irish Affairs and some Contemporary Documents. Large crown 8vo, printed on hand-made paper, parchment, 10s. 6d.

HENRY, Philip.—**Diaries and Letters of.** Edited by MATTHEW HENRY LEE, M.A. Large crown 8vo, 7s. 6d.

HINTON, J.—**Life and Letters.** With an Introduction by Sir W. W. GULL, Bart., and Portrait engraved on Steel by C. H. Jeens. Fifth Edition. Crown 8vo, 8s. 6d.

Philosophy and Religion. Selections from the Manuscripts of the late James Hinton. Edited by CAROLINE HADDON. Second Edition. Crown 8vo, 5s.

The Law Breaker, and The Coming of the Law. Edited by MARGARET HINTON. Crown 8vo, 6s.

The Mystery of Pain. New Edition. Fcap. 8vo, 1s.

Hodson of Hodson's Horse; or, Twelve Years of a Soldier's Life in India. Being extracts from the Letters of the late Major W. S. R. Hodson. With a Vindication from the Attack of Mr. Bosworth Smith. Edited by his brother, G. H. HODSON, M.A. Fourth Edition. Large crown 8vo, 5s.

HOLTHAM, E. G.—**Eight Years in Japan, 1873-1881.** Work, Travel, and Recreation. With three Maps. Large crown 8vo, 9s.

Homology of Economic Justice. An Essay by an East India Merchant. Small crown 8vo, 5*s*.

HOOPER, Mary.—**Little Dinners: How to Serve them with Elegance and Economy.** Twentieth Edition. Crown 8vo, 2*s*. 6*d*.

    Cookery for Invalids, Persons of Delicate Digestion, and Children. Fifth Edition. Crown 8vo, 2*s*. 6*d*.

    Every-Day Meals. Being Economical and Wholesome Recipes for Breakfast, Luncheon, and Supper. Sixth Edition. Crown 8vo, 2*s*. 6*d*.

HOPKINS, Ellice. — **Work amongst Working Men.** Sixth Edition. Crown 8vo, 3*s*. 6*d*.

HORNADAY, W. T.—**Two Years in a Jungle.** With Illustrations. Demy 8vo, 21*s*.

HOSPITALIER, E.—**The Modern Applications of Electricity.** Translated and Enlarged by JULIUS MAIER, Ph.D. 2 vols. Second Edition, Revised, with many additions and numerous Illustrations. Demy 8vo, 12*s*. 6*d*. each volume.
    VOL. I.—Electric Generators, Electric Light.
    VOL. II.—Telephone : Various Applications ; Electrical Transmission of Energy.

HOWARD, Robert, M.A.—**The Church of England and other Religious Communions.** A course of Lectures delivered in the Parish Church of Clapham. Crown 8vo, 7*s*. 6*d*.

HUMPHREY, Rev. William.—**The Bible and Belief.** A Letter to a Friend. Small Crown 8vo, 2*s*. 6*d*.

HUNTER, William C.—**Bits of Old China.** Small crown 8vo, 6*s*.

HUNTINGFORD, Rev. E., D.C.L.—**The Apocalypse.** With a Commentary and Introductory Essay. Demy 8vo, 5*s*.

HUTCHINSON, H.—**Thought Symbolism, and Grammatic Illusions.** Being a Treatise on the Nature, Purpose, and Material of Speech. Crown 8vo, 2*s*. 6*d*.

HUTTON, Rev. C. F.—**Unconscious Testimony ;** or, The Silent Witness of the Hebrew to the Truth of the Historical Scriptures. Crown 8vo, 2*s*. 6*d*.

HYNDMAN, H. M.—**The Historical Basis of Socialism in England.** Large crown 8vo, 8*s*. 6*d*.

IDDESLEIGH, Earl of.—**The Pleasures, Dangers, and Uses of Desultory Reading.** Fcap. 8vo, in Whatman paper cover, 1*s*.

IM THURN, Everard F.—**Among the Indians of Guiana.** Being Sketches, chiefly anthropologic, from the Interior of British Guiana. With 53 Illustrations and a Map. Demy 8vo, 18*s*.

JACCOUD, Prof. S.—The Curability and Treatment of Pulmonary Phthisis. Translated and edited by MONTAGU LUBBOCK, M.D. Demy 8vo, 15*s.*

Jaunt in a Junk : A Ten Days' Cruise in Indian Seas. Large crown 8vo, 7*s. 6d.*

JENKINS, E., and RAYMOND, J.—The Architect's Legal Handbook. Third Edition, revised. Crown 8vo, 6*s.*

JENKINS, Rev. Canon R. C.—Heraldry : English and Foreign. With a Dictionary of Heraldic Terms and 156 Illustrations. Small crown 8vo, 3*s. 6d.*

JERVIS, Rev. W. Henley.—The Gallican Church and the Revolution. A Sequel to the History of the Church of France, from the Concordat of Bologna to the Revolution. Demy 8vo, 18*s.*

JOEL, L.—A Consul's Manual and Shipowner's and Shipmaster's Practical Guide in their Transactions Abroad. With Definitions of Nautical, Mercantile, and Legal Terms ; a Glossary of Mercantile Terms in English, French, German, Italian, and Spanish ; Tables of the Money, Weights, and Measures of the Principal Commercial Nations and their Equivalents in British Standards ; and Forms of Consular and Notarial Acts. Demy 8vo, 12*s.*

JOHNSTON, H. H., F.Z.S.—The Kilima-njaro Expedition. A Record of Scientific Exploration in Eastern Equatorial Africa, and a General Description of the Natural History, Languages, and Commerce of the Kilima-njaro District. With 6 Maps, and over 80 Illustrations by the Author. Demy 8vo, 21*s.*

JOYCE, P. W., LL.D., etc.—Old Celtic Romances. Translated from the Gaelic. Crown 8vo, 7*s. 6d.*

KAUFMANN, Rev. M., B.A.—Socialism : its Nature, its Dangers, and its Remedies considered. Crown 8vo, 7*s. 6d.*

Utopias ; or, Schemes of Social Improvement, from Sir Thomas More to Karl Marx. Crown 8vo, 5*s.*

KAY, David, F.R.G.S.—Education and Educators. Crown 8vo, 7*s. 6d.*

KAY, Joseph.—Free Trade in Land. Edited by his Widow. With Preface by the Right Hon. JOHN BRIGHT, M.P. Seventh Edition. Crown 8vo, 5*s.*

  *** Also a cheaper edition, without the Appendix, but with a Revise of Recent Changes in the Land Laws of England, by the RIGHT HON. G. OSBORNE MORGAN, Q.C., M.P. Cloth, 1*s. 6d.* Paper covers, 1*s.*

KELKE, W. H. H.—An Epitome of English Grammar for the Use of Students. Adapted to the London Matriculation Course and Similar Examinations. Crown 8vo, 4*s. 6d.*

KEMPIS, Thomas à.—**Of the Imitation of Christ.** Parchment Library Edition.—Parchment or cloth, 6s. ; vellum, 7s. 6d. The Red Line Edition, fcap. 8vo, red edges, 2s. 6d. The Cabinet Edition, small 8vo, cloth limp, 1s. ; cloth boards, red edges, 1s. 6d. The Miniature Edition, red edges, 32mo, 1s.

*** All the above Editions may be had in various extra bindings.

KETTLEWELL, Rev. S.—**Thomas à Kempis and the Brothers of Common Life.** With Portrait. Crown 8vo, 7s. 6d.

KIDD, Joseph, M.D.—**The Laws of Therapeutics** ; or, the Science and Art of Medicine. Second Edition. Crown 8vo, 6s.

KINGSFORD, Anna, M.D.—**The Perfect Way in Diet.** A Treatise advocating a Return to the Natural and Ancient Food of our Race. Second Edition. Small crown 8vo, 2s.

KINGSLEY, Charles, M.A.—**Letters and Memories of his Life.** Edited by his Wife. With two Steel Engraved Portraits, and Vignettes on Wood. Fifteenth Cabinet Edition. 2 vols. Crown 8vo, 12s.

*** Also a People's Edition, in one volume. With Portrait. Crown 8vo, 6s.

All Saints' Day, and other Sermons. Edited by the Rev. W. HARRISON. Third Edition. Crown 8vo, 7s. 6d.

True Words for Brave Men. A Book for Soldiers' and Sailors' Libraries. Eleventh Edition. Crown 8vo, 2s. 6d.

KNOX, Alexander A.—**The New Playground** ; or, Wanderings in Algeria. New and Cheaper Edition. Large crown 8vo, 6s.

Land Concentration and Irresponsibility of Political Power, as causing the Anomaly of a Widespread State of Want by the Side of the Vast Supplies of Nature. Crown 8vo, 5s.

LANDON, Joseph.—**School Management** ; Including a General View of the Work of Education, Organization, and Discipline. Fifth Edition. Crown 8vo, 6s.

LEE, Rev. F. G., D.C.L.—**The Other World** ; or, Glimpses of the Supernatural. 2 vols. A New Edition. Crown 8vo, 15s.

Letters from an Unknown Friend. By the Author of "Charles Lowder." With a Preface by the Rev. W. H. CLEAVER. Fcap. 8vo, 1s.

Leward, Frank. Edited by CHARLES BAMPTON. Crown 8vo, 7s. 6d.

LEWIS, Edward Dillon.—**A Draft Code of Criminal Law and Procedure.** Demy 8vo, 21s.

Life of a Prig. By ONE. Third Edition. Fcap. 8vo, 3s. 6d.

LILLIE, Arthur, M.R.A.S.—**The Popular Life of Buddha.** Containing an Answer to the Hibbert Lectures of 1881. With Illustrations. Crown 8vo, 6s.

LLOYD, Walter.—**The Hope of the World :** An Essay on Universal Redemption. Crown 8vo, 5s.

LONGFELLOW, H. Wadsworth.—**Life.** By his Brother, SAMUEL LONGFELLOW. With Portraits and Illustrations. 2 vols. Demy 8vo, 28s.

LONSDALE, Margaret.—**Sister Dora :** a Biography. With Portrait. Cheap Edition. Small crown 8vo, 2s. 6d.

> **George Eliot: Thoughts upon her Life, her Books, and Herself.** Second Edition. Small crown 8vo, 1s. 6d.

LOUNSBURY, Thomas R.—**James Fenimore Cooper.** With Portrait. Crown 8vo, 5s.

LOWDER, Charles.—**A Biography.** By the Author of " St. Teresa." New and Cheaper Edition. Crown 8vo. With Portrait. 3s. 6d.

LÜCKES, Eva C. E.—**Lectures on General Nursing,** delivered to the Probationers of the London Hospital Training School for Nurses. Crown 8vo, 2s. 6d.

LYALL, William Rowe, D.D.—**Propædeia Prophetica ;** or, The Use and Design of the Old Testament Examined. New Edition. With Notices by GEORGE C. PEARSON, M.A., Hon. Canon of Canterbury. Demy 8vo, 10s. 6d.

LYTTON, Edward Bulwer, Lord.—**Life, Letters and Literary Remains.** By his Son, the EARL OF LYTTON. With Portraits, Illustrations and Facsimiles. Demy 8vo. Vols. I. and II., 32s.

MACAULAY, G. C.—**Francis Beaumont :** A Critical Study. Crown 8vo, 5s.

MAC CALLUM, M. W.—**Studies in Low German and High German Literature.** Crown 8vo, 6s.

MACHIAVELLI, Niccolò.—**Life and Times.** By Prof. VILLARI. Translated by LINDA VILLARI. 4 vols. Large post 8vo, 48s.

MACHIAVELLI, Niccolò.—**Discourses on the First Decade of Titus Livius.** Translated from the Italian by NINIAN HILL THOMSON, M.A. Large crown 8vo, 12s.

> **The Prince.** Translated from the Italian by N. H. T. Small crown 8vo, printed on hand-made paper, bevelled boards, 6s.

MACKENZIE, Alexander.—**How India is Governed.** Being an Account of England's Work in India. Small crown 8vo, 2s.

MAGNUS, Mrs.—**About the Jews since Bible Times.** From the Babylonian Exile till the English Exodus. Small crown 8vo, 6s.

MAGUIRE, Thomas.—**Lectures on Philosophy.** Demy 8vo, 9s.

MAIR, R. S., M.D., F.R.C.S.E.—**The Medical Guide for Anglo Indians.** Being a Compendium of Advice to Europe... India, relating to the Preservation and Regulation of With a Supplement on the Management of Chil... Second Edition. Crown 8vo, limp cloth, 3s. 6...

MALDEN, Henry Elliot.—**Vienna, 1683.** The History and Consequences of the Defeat of the Turks before Vienna, September 12th, 1683, by John Sobieski, King of Poland, and Charles Leopold, Duke of Lorraine. Crown 8vo, 4s. 6d.

Many Voices. A volume of Extracts from the Religious Writers of Christendom from the First to the Sixteenth Century. With Biographical Sketches. Crown 8vo, cloth extra, red edges, 6s.

MARKHAM, Capt. Albert Hastings, R.N.—**The Great Frozen Sea:** A Personal Narrative of the Voyage of the *Alert* during the Arctic Expedition of 1875-6. With 6 Full-page Illustrations, 2 Maps, and 27 Woodcuts. Sixth and Cheaper Edition. Crown 8vo, 6s.

MARTINEAU, Gertrude.—**Outline Lessons on Morals.** Small crown 8vo, 3s. 6d.

MAUDSLEY, H., M.D.—**Body and Will.** Being an Essay concerning Will, in its Metaphysical, Physiological, and Pathological Aspects. 8vo, 12s.

Natural Causes and Supernatural Seemings. Crown 8vo, 6s.

McGRATH, Terence.—**Pictures from Ireland.** New and Cheaper Edition. Crown 8vo, 2s.

MEREDITH, M.A.—**Theotokos, the Example for Woman.** Dedicated, by permission, to Lady Agnes Wood. Revised by the Venerable Archdeacon DENISON. 32mo, limp cloth, 1s. 6d.

MILLER, Edward.—**The History and Doctrines of Irvingism;** or, The so-called Catholic and Apostolic Church. 2 vols. Large post 8vo, 25s.

The Church in Relation to the State. Large crown 8vo, 7s. 6d.

MITCHELL, Lucy M.—**A History of Ancient Sculpture.** With numerous Illustrations, including 6 Plates in Phototype. Super royal 8vo, 42s.

MITFORD, Bertram.—**Through the Zulu Country.** Its Battlefields and its People. With Five Illustrations. Demy 8vo, 14s.

MOCKLER, E.—**A Grammar of the Baloochee Language, as** it is spoken in Makran (Ancient Gedrosia), in the Persia-Arabic and Roman characters. Fcap. 8vo, 5s.

MOLESWORTH, Rev. W. Nassau, M.A.—**History of the Church of England from 1660.** Large crown 8vo, 7s. 6d.

MORELL, J. R.—**Euclid Simplified in Method and Language.** Being a Manual of Geometry. Compiled from the most important French Works, approved by the University of Paris and the Minister of Public Instruction. Fcap. 8vo, 2s. 6d.

MORGAN, C. Lloyd.—**The Springs of Conduct.** An Essay in Evolution. Large crown 8vo, cloth, 7s. 6d.

MORRIS, George.—The Duality of all Divine Truth in our Lord Jesus Christ. For God's Self-manifestation in the Impartation of the Divine Nature to Man. Large crown 8vo, 7s. 6d.

MORSE, E. S., Ph.D.—First Book of Zoology. With numerous Illustrations. New and Cheaper Edition. Crown 8vo, 2s. 6d.

NELSON, J. H., M.A.—A Prospectus of the Scientific Study of the Hindû Law. Demy 8vo, 9s.

NEWMAN, Cardinal.—Characteristics from the Writings of. Being Selections from his various Works. Arranged with the Author's personal Approval. Seventh Edition. With Portrait. Crown 8vo, 6s.

** A Portrait of Cardinal Newman, mounted for framing, can be had, 2s. 6d.

NEWMAN, Francis William.—Essays on Diet. Small crown 8vo, cloth limp, 2s.

New Truth and the Old Faith: Are they Incompatible? By a Scientific Layman. Demy 8vo, 10s. 6d.

New Social Teachings. By POLITICUS. Small crown 8vo, 5s.

NICOLS, Arthur, F.G.S., F.R.G.S.—Chapters from the Physical History of the Earth: an Introduction to Geology and Palæontology. With numerous Illustrations. Crown 8vo, 5s.

NOEL, The Hon. Roden.—Essays on Poetry and Poets. Demy 8vo, 12s.

NOPS, Marianne.—Class Lessons on Euclid. Part I. containing the First Two Books of the Elements. Crown 8vo, 2s. 6d.

Nuces: EXERCISES ON THE SYNTAX OF THE PUBLIC SCHOOL LATIN PRIMER. New Edition in Three Parts. Crown 8vo, each 1s.

** The Three Parts can also be had bound together, 3s.

OATES, Frank, F.R.G.S.—Matabele Land and the Victoria Falls. A Naturalist's Wanderings in the Interior of South Africa. Edited by C. G. OATES, B.A. With numerous Illustrations and 4 Maps. Demy 8vo, 21s.

O'CONNOR, T. P., M.P.—The Parnell Movement. With a Sketch of Irish Parties from 1843. Large crown 8vo, 7s. 6d.

OGLE, W., M.D., F.R.C.P.—Aristotle on the Parts of Animals. Translated, with Introduction and Notes. Royal 8vo, 12s. 6d.

O'HAGAN, Lord, K.P.—Occasional Papers and Addresses. Large crown 8vo, 7s. 6d.

O'MEARA, Kathleen.—Frederic Ozanam, Professor of the Sorbonne: His Life and Work. Second Edition. Crown 8vo, 7s. 6d.

Henri Perreyve and his Counsels to the Sick. Small crown 8vo, 5s.

One and a Half in Norway. A Chronicle of Small Beer. By Either and Both. Small crown 8vo, 3s. 6d.

O'NEIL, the late Rev. Lord.—Sermons. With Memoir and Portrait. Crown 8vo, 6s.

Essays and Addresses. Crown 8vo, 5s.

Only Passport to Heaven, The. By One who has it. Small crown 8vo, 1s. 6d.

OSBORNE, Rev. W. A.—The Revised Version of the New Testament. A Critical Commentary, with Notes upon the Text. Crown 8vo, 5s.

OTTLEY, H. Bickersteth.—The Great Dilemma. Christ His Own Witness or His Own Accuser. Six Lectures. Second Edition. Crown 8vo, 3s. 6d.

Our Public Schools—Eton, Harrow, Winchester, Rugby, Westminster, Marlborough, The Charterhouse. Crown 8vo, 6s.

OWEN, F. M.—John Keats : a Study. Crown 8vo, 6s.

Across the Hills. Small crown 8vo, 1s. 6d.

OWEN, Rev. Robert, B.D.—Sanctorale Catholicum ; or, Book of Saints. With Notes, Critical, Exegetical, and Historical. Demy 8vo, 18s.

OXONIENSIS. — Romanism, Protestantism, Anglicanism. Being a Layman's View of some questions of the Day. Together with Remarks on Dr. Littledale's "Plain Reasons against joining the Church of Rome." Crown 8vo, 3s. 6d.

PALMER, the late William.—Notes of a Visit to Russia in 1840-1841. Selected and arranged by JOHN H. CARDINAL NEWMAN, with Portrait. Crown 8vo, 8s. 6d.

Early Christian Symbolism. A Series of Compositions from Fresco Paintings, Glasses, and Sculptured Sarcophagi. Edited by the Rev. Provost NORTHCOTE, D.D., and the Rev. Canon BROWNLOW, M.A. With Coloured Plates, folio, 42s., or with Plain Plates, folio, 25s.

Parchment Library. Choicely Printed on hand-made paper, limp parchment antique or cloth, 6s. ; vellum, 7s. 6d. each volume.

The Poetical Works of John Milton. 2 vols.

Letters and Journals of Jonathan Swift. Selected and edited, with a Commentary and Notes, by STANLEY LANE POOLE.

De Quincey's Confessions of an English Opium Eater. Reprinted from the First Edition. Edited by RICHARD GARNETT.

The Gospel according to Matthew, Mark, and Luke.

Parchment Library—*continued.*

Selections from the Prose Writings of Jonathan Swift. With a Preface and Notes by STANLEY LANE-POOLE and Portrait.

English Sacred Lyrics.

Sir Joshua Reynolds's Discourses. Edited by EDMUND GOSSE.

Selections from Milton's Prose Writings. Edited by ERNEST MYERS.

The Book of Psalms. Translated by the Rev. T. K. CHEYNE, M.A.

The Vicar of Wakefield. With Preface and Notes by AUSTIN DOBSON.

English Comic Dramatists. Edited by OSWALD CRAWFURD.

English Lyrics.

The Sonnets of John Milton. Edited by MARK PATTISON. With Portrait after Vertue.

French Lyrics. Selected and Annotated by GEORGE SAINTS-BURY. With a Miniature Frontispiece designed and etched by H. G. Glindoni.

Fables by Mr. John Gay. With Memoir by AUSTIN DOBSON, and an Etched Portrait from an unfinished Oil Sketch by Sir Godfrey Kneller.

Select Letters of Percy Bysshe Shelley. Edited, with an Introduction, by RICHARD GARNETT.

The Christian Year. Thoughts in Verse for the Sundays and Holy Days throughout the Year. With Miniature Portrait of the Rev. J. Keble, after a Drawing by G. Richmond, R.A.

Shakspere's Works. Complete in Twelve Volumes.

Eighteenth Century Essays. Selected and Edited by AUSTIN DOBSON. With a Miniature Frontispiece by R. Caldecott.

Q. Horati Flacci Opera. Edited by F. A. CORNISH, Assistant Master at Eton. With a Frontispiece after a design by L. Alma Tadema, etched by Leopold Lowenstam.

Edgar Allan Poe's Poems. With an Essay on his Poetry by ANDREW LANG, and a Frontispiece by Linley Sambourne.

Shakspere's Sonnets. Edited by EDWARD DOWDEN. With a Frontispiece etched by Leopold Lowenstam, after the Death Mask.

English Odes. Selected by EDMUND GOSSE. With Frontispiece on India paper by Hamo Thornycroft, A.R.A.

Parchment Library—*continued.*

Of the Imitation of Christ. By Thomas à Kempis. A revised Translation. With Frontispiece on India paper, from a Design by W. B. Richmond.

Poems: Selected from Percy Bysshe Shelley. Dedicated to Lady Shelley. With a Preface by Richard Garnett and a Miniature Frontispiece.

PARSLOE, *Joseph.*—Our Railways. Sketches, Historical and Descriptive. With Practical Information as to Fares and Rates, etc., and a Chapter on Railway Reform. Crown 8vo, 6s.

PASCAL, *Blaise.*—The Thoughts of. Translated from the Text of Auguste Molinier, by C. Kegan Paul. Large crown 8vo, with Frontispiece, printed on hand-made paper, parchment antique, or cloth, 12s.; vellum, 15s.

PAUL, *Alexander.*—Short Parliaments. A History of the National Demand for frequent General Elections. Small crown 8vo, 3s. 6d.

PAUL, C. *Kegan.*—Biographical Sketches. Printed on hand-made paper, bound in buckram. Second Edition. Crown 8vo, 7s. 6d.

PEARSON, *Rev. S.*—Week-day Living. A Book for Young Men and Women. Second Edition. Crown 8vo, 5s.

PENRICE, *Major J.*—Arabic and English Dictionary of the Koran. 4to, 21s.

PESCHEL, *Dr. Oscar.*—The Races of Man and their Geographical Distribution. Second Edition. Large crown 8vo, 9s.

PHIPSON, *E.*—The Animal Lore of Shakspeare's Time. Including Quadrupeds, Birds, Reptiles, Fish and Insects. Large post 8vo, 9s.

PIDGEON, *D.*—An Engineer's Holiday; or, Notes of a Round Trip from Long. o° to o°. New and Cheaper Edition. Large crown 8vo, 7s. 6d.

Old World Questions and New World Answers. Second Edition. Large crown 8vo, 7s. 6d.

Plain Thoughts for Men. Eight Lectures delivered at Forester's Hall, Clerkenwell, during the London Mission, 1884. Crown 8vo, cloth, 1s. 6d; paper covers, 1s.

POE, *Edgar Allan.*—Works of. With an Introduction and a Memoir by Richard Henry Stoddard. In 6 vols. With Frontispieces and Vignettes. Large crown 8vo, 6s. each.

POPE, *J. Buckingham.* — Railway Rates and Radical Rule. Trade Questions as Election Tests. Crown 8vo, 2s. 6d.

PRICE, *Prof. Bonamy.* — Chapters on Practical Political Economy. Being the Substance of Lectures delivered before the University of Oxford. New and Cheaper Edition. Crown 8vo, 5s.

Pulpit Commentary, The. (Old Testament Series.) Edited by the Rev. J. S. EXELL, M.A., and the Rev. Canon H. D. M. SPENCE.

> **Genesis.** By the Rev. T. WHITELAW, M.A. With Homilies by the Very Rev. J. F. MONTGOMERY, D.D., Rev. Prof. R. A. REDFORD, M.A., LL.B., Rev. F. HASTINGS, Rev. W. ROBERTS, M.A. An Introduction to the Study of the Old Testament by the Venerable Archdeacon FARRAR, D.D., F.R.S.; and Introductions to the Pentateuch by the Right Rev. H. COTTERILL, D.D., and Rev. T. WHITELAW, M.A. Eighth Edition. 1 vol., 15s.

> **Exodus.** By the Rev. Canon RAWLINSON. With Homilies by Rev. J. ORR, Rev. D. YOUNG, B.A., Rev. C. A. GOODHART, Rev. J. URQUHART, and the Rev. H. T. ROBJOHNS. Fourth Edition. 2 vols., 18s.

> **Leviticus.** By the Rev. Prebendary MEYRICK, M.A. With Introductions by the Rev. R. COLLINS, Rev. Professor A. CAVE, and Homilies by Rev. Prof. REDFORD, LL.B., Rev. J. A. MACDONALD, Rev. W. CLARKSON, B.A., Rev. S. R. ALDRIDGE, LL.B., and Rev. McCHEYNE EDGAR. Fourth Edition. 15s.

> **Numbers.** By the Rev. R. WINTERBOTHAM, LL.B. With Homilies by the Rev. Professor W. BINNIE, D.D., Rev. E. S. PROUT, M.A., Rev. D. YOUNG, Rev. J. WAITE, and an Introduction by the Rev. THOMAS WHITELAW, M.A. Fourth Edition. 15s.

> **Deuteronomy.** By the Rev. W. L. ALEXANDER, D.D. With Homilies by Rev. C. CLEMANCE, D.D., Rev. J. ORR, B.D., Rev. R. M. EDGAR, M.A., Rev. D. DAVIES, M.A. Fourth edition. 15s.

> **Joshua.** By Rev. J. J. LIAS, M.A. With Homilies by Rev. S. R. ALDRIDGE, LL.B., Rev. R. GLOVER, REV. E. DE PRESSENSÉ, D.D., Rev. J. WAITE, B.A., Rev. W. F. ADENEY, M.A.; and an Introduction by the Rev. A. PLUMMER, M.A. Fifth Edition. 12s. 6d.

> **Judges and Ruth.** By the Bishop of Bath and Wells, and Rev. J. MORISON, D.D. With Homilies by Rev. A. F. MUIR, M.A., Rev. W. F. ADENEY, M.A., Rev. W. M. STATHAM, and Rev. Professor J. THOMSON, M.A. Fifth Edition. 10s. 6d.

> **1 Samuel.** By the Very Rev. R. P. SMITH, D.D. With Homilies by Rev. DONALD FRASER, D.D., Rev. Prof. CHAPMAN, and Rev. B. DALE. Sixth Edition. 15s.

> **1 Kings.** By the Rev. JOSEPH HAMMOND, LL.B. With Homilies by the Rev. E. DE PRESSENSÉ, D.D., Rev. J. WAITE, B.A., Rev. A. ROWLAND, LL.B., Rev. J. A. MACDONALD, and Rev. J. URQUHART. Fourth Edition. 15s.

Pulpit Commentary, The—*continued.*

1 Chronicles. By the Rev. Prof. P. C. BARKER, M.A., LL.B. With Homilies by Rev. Prof. J. R. THOMSON, M.A., Rev. R. TUCK, B.A., Rev. W. CLARKSON, B.A., Rev. F. WHITFIELD, M.A., and Rev. RICHARD GLOVER. 15*s*.

Ezra, Nehemiah, and Esther. By Rev. Canon G. RAWLINSON, M.A. With Homilies by Rev. Prof. J. R. THOMSON, M.A., Rev. Prof. R. A. REDFORD, LL.B., M.A., Rev. W. S. LEWIS, M.A., Rev. J. A. MACDONALD, Rev. A. MACKENNAL, B.A., Rev. W. CLARKSON, B.A., Rev. F. HASTINGS, Rev. W. DINWIDDIE, LL.B., Rev. Prof. ROWLANDS, B.A., Rev. G. WOOD, B.A., Rev. Prof. P. C. BARKER, M.A., LL.B., and the Rev. J. S. EXELL, M.A. Sixth Edition. 1 vol., 12*s*. 6*d*.

Jeremiah. (Vol. I.) By the Rev. T. K. CHEYNE, M.A. With Homilies by the Rev. W. F. ADENEY, M.A., Rev. A. F. MUIR, M.A., Rev. S. CONWAY, B.A., Rev. J. WAITE, B.A., and Rev. D. YOUNG, B.A. Second Edition. 15*s*.

Jeremiah (Vol. II.) and Lamentations. By Rev. T. K. CHEYNE, M.A. With Homilies by Rev. Prof. J. R. THOMSON, M.A., Rev. W. F. ADENEY, M.A., Rev. A. F. MUIR, M.A., Rev. S. CONWAY, B.A., Rev. D. YOUNG, B.A. 15*s*.

Pulpit Commentary, The. (New Testament Series.)

St. Mark. By Very Rev. E. BICKERSTETH, D.D., Dean of Lichfield. With Homilies by Rev. Prof. THOMSON, M.A., Rev. Prof. GIVEN, M.A., Rev. Prof. JOHNSON, M.A., Rev. A. ROWLAND, B.A., LL.B., Rev. A. MUIR, and Rev. R. GREEN. Fifth Edition. 2 vols., 21*s*.

The Acts of the Apostles. By the Bishop of Bath and Wells. With Homilies by Rev. Prof. P. C. BARKER, M.A., LL.B., Rev. Prof. E. JOHNSON, M.A., Rev. Prof. R. A. REDFORD, M.A., Rev. R. TUCK, B.A., Rev. W. CLARKSON, B.A. Third Edition. 2 vols., 21*s*.

I. Corinthians. By the Ven. Archdeacon FARRAR, D.D. With Homilies by Rev. Ex-Chancellor LIPSCOMB, LL.D., Rev. DAVID THOMAS, D.D., Rev. D. FRASER, D.D., Rev. Prof. J. R. THOMSON, M.A., Rev. J. WAITE, B.A., Rev. R. TUCK, B.A., Rev. E. HURNDALL, M.A., and Rev. H. BREMNER, B.D. Third Edition. Price 15*s*.

II. Corinthians and Galatians. By the Ven. Archdeacon FARRAR, D.D., and Rev. Preb. E. HUXTABLE. With Homilies by Rev. Ex-Chancellor LIPSCOMB, LL.D., Rev. DAVID THOMAS, D.D., Rev. DONALD FRASER, D.D., Rev. R. TUCK, B.A., Rev. E. HURNDALL, M.A., Rev. Prof. J. R. THOMSON, M.A., Rev. R. FINLAYSON, B.A., Rev. W. F. ADENEY, M.A., Rev. R. M. EDGAR, M.A., and Rev. T. CROSKERRY, D.D. Price 21*s*.

Pulpit Commentary, The. (New Testament Series.)—*continued.*

    Ephesians, Phillipians, and Colossians. By the Rev. Prof.
W. G. BLAIKIE, D.D., Rev. B. C. CAFFIN, M.A., and Rev. G.
G. FINDLAY, B.A. With Homilies by Rev. D. THOMAS, D.D.,
Rev. R. M. EDGAR, M.A., Rev. R. FINLAYSON, B.A., Rev.
W. F. ADENEY, M.A., Rev. Prof. T. CROSKERRY, D.D., Rev.
E. S. PROUT, M.A., Rev. Canon VERNON HUTTON, and
Rev. U. R. THOMAS, D.D. Price 21s.

    Hebrews and James. By the Rev. J. BARNBY, D.D., and Rev.
Prebendary E. C. S. GIBSON, M.A. With Homiletics by the
Rev. C. JERDAN, M.A., LL.B., and Rev. Prebendary E. C. S.
GIBSON. And Homilies by the Rev. W. JONES, Rev. C. NEW,
Rev. D. YOUNG, B.A., Rev. J. S. BRIGHT, Rev. T. F. LOCKYER,
B.A., and Rev. C. JERDAN, M.A., LL.B. Price 15s.

PUNCHARD, E. G., D.D.—**Christ of Contention.** Three Essays.
Fcap. 8vo, 2s.

PUSEY, Dr.—**Sermons for the Church's Seasons from
Advent to Trinity.** Selected from the Published Sermons
of the late EDWARD BOUVERIE PUSEY, D.D. Crown 8vo, 5s.

RANKE, Leopold von.—**Universal History.** The oldest Historical
Group of Nations and the Greeks. Edited by G. W. PROTHERO.
Demy 8vo, 16s.

RENDELL, J. M.—**Concise Handbook of the Island of
Madeira.** With Plan of Funchal and Map of the Island. Fcap.
8vo, 1s. 6d.

REYNOLDS, Rev. J. W.—**The Supernatural in Nature.** A
Verification by Free Use of Science. Third Edition, Revised
and Enlarged. Demy 8vo, 14s.

    The Mystery of Miracles. Third and Enlarged Edition.
Crown 8vo, 6s.

    The Mystery of the Universe; Our Common Faith. Demy
8vo, 14s.

RIBOT, Prof. Th.—**Heredity:** A Psychological Study on its Phenomena,
its Laws, its Causes, and its Consequences. Second Edition.
Large crown 8vo, 9s.

RIMMER, William, M.D.—**Art Anatomy.** A Portfolio of 81 Plates.
Folio, 70s., nett.

ROBERTSON, The late Rev. F. W., M.A.—**Life and Letters of.**
Edited by the Rev. STOPFORD BROOKE, M.A.

    I. Two vols., uniform with the Sermons. With Steel Portrait.
Crown 8vo, 7s. 6d.

    II. Library Edition, in Demy 8vo, with Portrait. 12s.

    III. A Popular Edition, in 1 vol. Crown 8vo, 6s.

    Sermons. Four Series. Small crown 8vo, 3s. 6d. each.

    The Human Race, and other Sermons. Preached at Cheltenham, Oxford, and Brighton. New and Cheaper Edition. Small
crown 8vo, 3s. 6d.

ROBERTSON, The late Rev. F. W., M.A.—continued.

Notes on Genesis. New and Cheaper Edition. Small crown 8vo, 3s. 6d.

Expository Lectures on St. Paul's Epistles to the Corinthians. A New Edition. Small crown 8vo, 5s.

Lectures and Addresses, with other Literary Remains. A New Edition. Small crown 8vo, 5s.

An Analysis of Tennyson's " In Memoriam." (Dedicated by Permission to the Poet-Laureate.) Fcap. 8vo, 2s.

The Education of the Human Race. Translated from the German of GOTTHOLD EPHRAIM LESSING. Fcap. 8vo, 2s. 6d.

The above Works can also be had, bound in half morocco.

*** A Portrait of the late Rev. F. W. Robertson, mounted for framing, can be had, 2s. 6d.

ROMANES, G. J. — **Mental Evolution in Animals.** With a Posthumous Essay on Instinct by CHARLES DARWIN, F.R.S. Demy 8vo, 12s.

ROOSEVELT, Theodore. **Hunting Trips of a Ranchman.** Sketches of Sport on the Northern Cattle Plains. With 26 Illustrations. Royal 8vo, 18s.

Rosmini's Origin of Ideas. Translated from the Fifth Italian Edition of the Nuovo Saggio *Sull' origine delle idee.* 3 vols. Demy 8vo, cloth, 16s. each.

Rosmini's Psychology. 3 vols. Demy 8vo. [Vols. I. and II. now ready, 16s. each.

Rosmini's Philosophical System. Translated, with a Sketch of the Author's Life, Bibliography, Introduction, and Notes by THOMAS DAVIDSON. Demy 8vo, 16s.

RULE, Martin, M.A. — **The Life and Times of St. Anselm, Archbishop of Canterbury and Primate of the Britains.** 2 vols. Demy 8vo, 32s.

SAMUEL, Sydney M.—**Jewish Life in the East.** Small crown 8vo, 3s. 6d.

SARTORIUS, Ernestine.—**Three Months in the Soudan.** With 11 Full-page Illustrations. Demy 8vo, 14s.

SAYCE, Rev. Archibald Henry.—**Introduction to the Science of Language.** 2 vols. Second Edition. Large post 8vo, 21s.

SCOONES, W. Baptiste.—**Four Centuries of English Letters:** A Selection of 350 Letters by 150 Writers, from the Period of the Paston Letters to the Present Time. Third Edition. Large crown 8vo, 6s.

SÉE, Prof. Germain.—**Bacillary Phthisis of the Lungs.** Translated and edited for English Practitioners by WILLIAM HENRY WEDDELL, M.R.C.S. Demy 8vo, 10s. 6d.

Shakspere's Works. The Avon Edition, 12 vols., fcap. 8vo, cloth, 18s. ; in cloth box, 21s. ; bound in 6 vols., cloth, 15s.

SHILLITO, Rev. Joseph.—**Womanhood** : its Duties, Temptations, and Privileges. A Book for Young Women. Third Edition. Crown 8vo, 3s. 6d.

SIDNEY, Algernon.—**A Review.** By GERTRUDE M. IRELAND BLACK-BURNE. Crown 8vo, 6s.

Sister Augustine, Superior of the Sisters of Charity at the St. Johannis Hospital at Bonn. Authorised Translation by HANS THARAU, from the German "Memorials of AMALIE VON LASAULX." Cheap Edition. Large crown 8vo, 4s. 6d.

SKINNER, James.—**A Memoir.** By the Author of "Charles Lowder." With a Preface by the Rev. Canon CARTER, and Portrait. Large crown, 7s. 6d.
　　 *** Also a cheap Edition. With Portrait. Crown 8vo, 3s. 6d.

SMITH, Edward, M.D., LL.B., F.R.S.—**Tubercular Consumption in its Early and Remediable Stages.** Second Edition. Crown 8vo, 6s.

SMITH, Sir W. Cusack, Bart.—**Our War Ships.** A Naval Essay. Crown 8vo, 5s.

Spanish Mystics. By the Editor of "Many Voices." Crown 8vo, 5s.

Specimens of English Prose Style from Malory to Macaulay. Selected and Annotated, with an Introductory Essay, by GEORGE SAINTSBURY. Large crown 8vo, printed on hand-made paper, parchment antique or cloth, 12s. ; vellum, 15s.

SPEDDING, James.—**Reviews and Discussions, Literary, Political, and Historical not relating to Bacon.** Demy 8vo, 12s. 6d.

　　 Evenings with a Reviewer; or, Macaulay and Bacon. With a Prefatory Notice by G. S. VENABLES, Q.C. 2 vols. Demy 8vo, 18s.

STAPFER, Paul.—**Shakespeare and Classical Antiquity** : Greek and Latin Antiquity as presented in Shakespeare's Plays. Translated by EMILY J. CAREY. Large post 8vo, 12s.

STATHAM, F. Reginald.—**Free Thought and Truth Thought.** A Contribution to an Existing Argument. Crown 8vo, 6s.

STEVENSON, Rev. W. F.—**Hymns for the Church and Home.** Selected and Edited by the Rev. W. FLEMING STEVENSON.
　　 The Hymn Book consists of Three Parts :—I. For Public Worship.—II. For Family and Private Worship.—III. For Children. SMALL EDITION. Cloth limp, 10d. ; cloth boards, 1s. LARGE TYPE EDITION. Cloth limp, 1s. 3d. ; cloth boards, 1s. 6d.

Stray Papers on Education, and Scenes from School Life. By B. H. Second Edition. Small crown 8vo, 3s. 6d.

STREATFEILD, Rev. G. S., M.A.—**Lincolnshire and the Danes.** Large crown 8vo, 7s. 6d.

STRECKER-WISLICENUS.—**Organic Chemistry.** Translated and Edited, with Extensive Additions, by W. R. HODGKINSON, Ph.D., and A. J. GREENAWAY, F.I.C. Second and cheaper Edition. Demy 8vo, 12s. 6d.

Suakin, 1885; being a Sketch of the Campaign of this year. By an Officer who was there. Second Edition. Crown 8vo, 2s. 6d.

SULLY, James, M.A.—**Pessimism : a History and a Criticism.** Second Edition. Demy 8vo, 14s.

Sunshine and Sea. A Yachting Visit to the Channel Islands and Coast of Brittany. With Frontispiece from a Photograph and 24 Illustrations. Crown 8vo, 6s.

SWEDENBORG, Eman.—**De Cultu et Amore Dei ubi Agitur de Telluris ortu, Paradiso et Vivario, tum de Primogeniti Seu Adami Nativitate Infantia, et Amore.** Crown 8vo, 6s.

  On the Worship and Love of God. Treating of the Birth of the Earth, Paradise, and the Abode of Living Creatures. Translated from the original Latin. Crown 8vo, 7s. 6d.

  Prodromus Philosophiæ Ratiocinantis de Infinito, et Causa Finali Creationis : deque Mechanismo Operationis Animæ et Corporis. Edidit THOMAS MURRAY GORMAN, M.A. Crown 8vo, 7s. 6d.

TACITUS.—**The Agricola.** A Translation. Small crown 8vo, 2s. 6d.

TAYLOR, Rev. Isaac.—**The Alphabet.** An Account of the Origin and Development of Letters. With numerous Tables and Facsimiles. 2 vols. Demy 8vo, 36s.

TAYLOR, Jeremy.—**The Marriage Ring.** With Preface, Notes, and Appendices. Edited by FRANCIS BURDETT MONEY COUTTS. Small crown 8vo, 2s. 6d.

TAYLOR, Sedley. — **Profit Sharing between Capital and Labour.** To which is added a Memorandum on the Industrial Partnership at the Whitwood Collieries, by ARCHIBALD and HENRY BRIGGS, with remarks by SEDLEY TAYLOR. Crown 8vo, 2s. 6d.

"They Might Have Been Together Till the Last." An Essay on Marriage, and the position of Women in England. Small crown 8vo, 2s.

Thirty Thousand Thoughts. Edited by the Rev. CANON SPENCE, Rev. J. S. EXELL, and Rev. CHARLES NEIL. 6 vols. Super royal 8vo.

        [Vols. I.–IV. now ready, 16s. each.

THOM, J. Hamilton.—**Laws of Life after the Mind of Christ.** Two Series. Crown 8vo, 7s. 6d. each.

THOMPSON, Sir H.—**Diet in Relation to Age and Activity.** Fcap. 8vo, cloth, 1s. 6d. ; Paper covers, 1s.

TIPPLE, Rev. S. A.—Sunday Mornings at Norwood. Prayers and Sermons. Crown 8vo, 6s.

TODHUNTER, Dr. J.—A Study of Shelley. Crown 8vo, 7s.

TOLSTOI, Count Leo.—Christ's Christianity. Translated from the Russian. Large crown 8vo, 7s. 6d.

TRANT, William.—Trade Unions : Their Origin, Objects, and Efficacy. Small crown 8vo, 1s. 6d. ; paper covers, 1s.

TREMENHEERE, Hugh Seymour, C.B.— A Manual of the Principles of Government, as set forth by the Authorities of Ancient and Modern Times. New and Enlarged Edition. Crown 8vo, 3s. 6d. Cheap Edition, limp cloth, 1s.

TRENCH, The late R. C., Archbishop.—Notes on the Parables of Our Lord. Fourteenth Edition. 8vo, 12s.

Notes on the Miracles of Our Lord. Twelfth Edition. 8vo, 12s.

Studies in the Gospels. Fifth Edition, Revised. 8vo, 10s. 6d.

Brief Thoughts and Meditations on Some Passages in Holy Scripture. Third Edition. Crown 8vo, 3s. 6d.

Synonyms of the New Testament. Ninth Edition, Enlarged. 8vo, 12s.

Selected Sermons. Crown 8vo, 6s.

On the Authorized Version of the New Testament. Second Edition. 8vo, 7s.

Commentary on the Epistles to the Seven Churches in Asia. Fourth Edition, Revised. 8vo, 8s. 6d.

The Sermon on the Mount. An Exposition drawn from the Writings of St. Augustine, with an Essay on his Merits as an Interpreter of Holy Scripture. Fourth Edition, Enlarged. 8vo, 10s. 6d.

Shipwrecks of Faith. Three Sermons preached before the University of Cambridge in May, 1867. Fcap. 8vo, 2s. 6d.

Lectures on Mediæval Church History. Being the Substance of Lectures delivered at Queen's College, London. Second Edition. 8vo, 12s.

English, Past and Present. Thirteenth Edition, Revised and Improved. Fcap. 8vo, 5s.

On the Study of Words. Nineteenth Edition, Revised. Fcap. 8vo, 5s.

Select Glossary of English Words Used Formerly in Senses Different from the Present. Fifth Edition, Revised and Enlarged. Fcap. 8vo, 5s.

Proverbs and Their Lessons. Seventh Edition, Enlarged. Fcap. 8vo, 4s.

Poems. Collected and Arranged anew. Ninth Edition. Fcap. 8vo, 7s. 6d.

TRENCH, The late R. C., Archbishop.—continued.

Poems. Library Edition. 2 vols. Small crown 8vo, 10s.

Sacred Latin Poetry. Chiefly Lyrical, Selected and Arranged for Use. Third Edition, Corrected and Improved. Fcap. 8vo, 7s.

A Household Book of English Poetry. Selected and Arranged, with Notes. Fourth Edition, Revised. Extra fcap. 8vo, 5s. 6d.

An Essay on the Life and Genius of Calderon. With Translations from his "Life's a Dream" and "Great Theatre of the World." Second Edition, Revised and Improved. Extra fcap. 8vo, 5s. 6d.

Gustavus Adolphus in Germany, and other Lectures on the Thirty Years' War. Second Edition, Enlarged. Fcap. 8vo, 4s.

Plutarch: his Life, his Lives, and his Morals. Second Edition, Enlarged. Fcap. 8vo, 3s. 6d.

Remains of the late Mrs. Richard Trench. Being Selections from her Journals, Letters, and other Papers. New and Cheaper Issue. With Portrait. 8vo, 6s.

TUKE, Daniel Hack, M.D., F.R.C.P. Chapters in the History of the Insane in the British Isles. With Four Illustrations. Large crown 8vo, 12s.

TWINING, Louisa.—Workhouse Visiting and Management during Twenty-Five Years. Small crown 8vo, 2s.

TYLER, J.—The Mystery of Being: or, What Do We Know? Small crown 8vo, 3s. 6d.

VAUGHAN, H. Halford.—New Readings and Renderings of Shakespeare's Tragedies. 3 vols. Demy 8vo, 12s. 6d. each.

VILLARI, Professor.—Niccolò Machiavelli and his Times. Translated by LINDA VILLARI. 4 vols. Large post 8vo, 48s.

VILLIERS, The Right Hon. C. P.—Free Trade Speeches of. With Political Memoir. Edited by a Member of the Cobden Club. 2 vols. With Portrait. Demy 8vo, 25s.

*** People's Edition. 1 vol. Crown 8vo, limp cloth, 2s. 6d.

VOGT, Lieut.-Col. Hermann.—The Egyptian War of 1882. A translation. With Map and Plans. Large crown 8vo, 6s.

VOLCKXSOM, E. W. v.—Catechism of Elementary Modern Chemistry. Small crown 8vo, 3s.

WALLER, Rev. C. B.—The Apocalypse, reviewed under the Light of the Doctrine of the Unfolding Ages, and the Restitution of All Things. Demy 8vo, 12s.

The Bible Record of Creation viewed in its Letter and Spirit. Two Sermons preached at St. Paul's Church, Woodford Bridge. Crown 8vo, 1s. 6d.

WALPOLE, Chas. George.—A Short History of Ireland from the Earliest Times to the Union with Great Britain. With 5 Maps and Appendices. Second Edition. Crown 8vo, 6s.

WARD, William George, Ph.D.—Essays on the Philosophy of Theism. Edited, with an Introduction, by WILFRID WARD. 2 vols. Demy 8vo, 21s.

WARD, Wilfrid.—The Wish to Believe. A Discussion Concerning the Temper of Mind in which a reasonable Man should undertake Religious Inquiry. Small crown 8vo, 5s.

WARTER, J. W.—An Old Shropshire Oak. 2 vols. Demy 8vo, 28s.

WEDDERBURN, Sir David, Bart., M.P.—Life of. Compiled from his Journals and Writings by his sister, Mrs. E. H. PERCIVAL. With etched Portrait, and facsimiles of Pencil Sketches. Demy 8vo, 14s.

WEDMORE, Frederick.—The Masters of Genre Painting. With Sixteen Illustrations. Post 8vo, 7s. 6d.

WHITE, R. E.—Recollections of Woolwich during the Crimean War and Indian Mutiny, and of the Ordnance and War Departments ; together with complete Lists of Past and Present Officials of the Royal Arsenal, etc. Crown 8vo, 2s. 6d.

WHITNEY, Prof. William Dwight.—Essentials of English Grammar, for the Use of Schools. Second Edition. Crown 8vo, 3s. 6d.

WHITWORTH, George Clifford.—An Anglo-Indian Dictionary : a Glossary of Indian Terms used in English, and of such English or other Non-Indian Terms as have obtained special meanings in India. Demy 8vo, cloth, 12s.

WILLIAMS, Rowland, D.D.—Psalms, Litanies, Counsels, and Collects for Devout Persons. Edited by his Widow. New and Popular Edition. Crown 8vo, 3s. 6d.

Stray Thoughts from the Note Books of the late Rowland Williams, D.D. Edited by his Widow. Crown 8vo, 3s. 6d.

WILSON, Lieut.-Col. C. T.— The Duke of Berwick, Marshal of France, 1702-1734. Demy 8vo, 15s.

WILSON, Mrs. R. F.—The Christian Brothers. Their Origin and Work. With a Sketch of the Life of their Founder, the Ven. JEAN BAPTISTE, de la Salle. Crown 8vo, 6s.

WOLTMANN, Dr. Alfred, and WOERMANN, Dr. Karl.—History of Painting. With numerous Illustrations. Vol. I. Painting in Antiquity and the Middle Ages. Medium 8vo, 28s., bevelled boards, gilt leaves, 30s. Vol. II. The Painting of the Renascence.

YOUMANS, Eliza A.—**First Book of Botany.** Designed to Cultivate the Observing Powers of Children. With 300 Engravings. New and Cheaper Edition. Crown 8vo, 2s. 6d.

YOUMANS, Edward L., M.D.—**A Class Book of Chemistry,** on the Basis of the New System. With 200 Illustrations. Crown 8vo, 5s.

THE INTERNATIONAL SCIENTIFIC SERIES.

I. **Forms of Water:** a Familiar Exposition of the Origin and Phenomena of Glaciers. By J. Tyndall, LL.D., F.R.S. With 25 Illustrations. Ninth Edition. 5s.

II. **Physics and Politics;** or, Thoughts on the Application of the Principles of "Natural Selection" and "Inheritance" to Political Society. By Walter Bagehot. Seventh Edition. 4s.

III. **Foods.** By Edward Smith, M.D., LL.B., F.R.S. With numerous Illustrations. Eighth Edition. 5s.

IV. **Mind and Body:** the Theories of their Relation. By Alexander Bain, LL.D. With Four Illustrations. Seventh Edition. 4s.

V. **The Study of Sociology.** By Herbert Spencer. Twelfth Edition. 5s.

VI. **On the Conservation of Energy.** By Balfour Stewart, M.A., LL.D., F.R.S. With 14 Illustrations. Sixth Edition. 5s.

VII. **Animal Locomotion;** or Walking, Swimming, and Flying. By J. B. Pettigrew, M.D., F.R.S., etc. With 130 Illustrations. Third Edition. 5s.

VIII. **Responsibility in Mental Disease.** By Henry Maudsley, M.D. Fourth Edition. 5s.

IX. **The New Chemistry.** By Professor J. P. Cooke. With 31 Illustrations. Eighth Edition, remodelled and enlarged. 5s.

X. **The Science of Law.** By Professor Sheldon Amos. Sixth Edition. 5s.

XI. **Animal Mechanism:** a Treatise on Terrestrial and Aerial Locomotion. By Professor E. J. Marey. With 117 Illustrations. Third Edition. 5s.

XII. **The Doctrine of Descent and Darwinism.** By Professor Oscar Schmidt. With 26 Illustrations. Sixth Edition. 5s.

XIII. **The History of the Conflict between Religion and Science.** By J. W. Draper, M.D., LL.D. Nineteenth Edition. 5s.

XIV. **Fungi:** their Nature, Influences, Uses, etc. By M. C. Cooke, M.D., LL.D. Edited by the Rev. M. J. Berkeley, M.A., F.L.S. With numerous Illustrations. Third Edition. 5s.

XV. **The Chemical Effects of Light and Photography.** By Dr. Hermann Vogel. With 100 Illustrations. Fourth Edition. 5*s.*

XVI. **The Life and Growth of Language.** By Professor William Dwight Whitney. Fifth Edition. 5*s.*

XVII. **Money and the Mechanism of Exchange.** By W. Stanley Jevons, M.A., F.R.S. Seventh Edition. 5*s.*

XVIII. **The Nature of Light.** With a General Account of Physical Optics. By Dr. Eugene Lommel. With 188 Illustrations and a Table of Spectra in Chromo-lithography. Third Edition. 5*s.*

XIX. **Animal Parasites and Messmates.** By P. J. Van Beneden. With 83 Illustrations. Third Edition. 5*s.*

XX. **Fermentation.** By Professor Schützenberger. With 28 Illustrations. Fourth Edition. 5*s.*

XXI. **The Five Senses of Man.** By Professor Bernstein. With 91 Illustrations. Fifth Edition. 5*s.*

XXII. **The Theory of Sound in its Relation to Music.** By Professor Pietro Blaserna. With numerous Illustrations. Third Edition. 5*s.*

XXIII. **Studies in Spectrum Analysis.** By J. Norman Lockyer, F.R.S. With six photographic Illustrations of Spectra, and numerous engravings on Wood. Third Edition. 6*s.* 6*d.*

XXIV. **A History of the Growth of the Steam Engine.** By Professor R. H. Thurston. With numerous Illustrations. Third Edition. 6*s.* 6*d.*

XXV. **Education as a Science.** By Alexander Bain, LL.D. Fifth Edition. 5*s.*

XXVI. **The Human Species.** By Professor A. de Quatrefages. Third Edition. 5*s.*

XXVII. **Modern Chromatics.** With Applications to Art and Industry. By Ogden N. Rood. With 130 original Illustrations. Second Edition. 5*s.*

XXVIII. **The Crayfish : an Introduction to the Study of Zoology.** By Professor T. H. Huxley. With 82 Illustrations. Fourth Edition. 5*s.*

XXIX. **The Brain as an Organ of Mind.** By H. Charlton Bastian, M.D. With numerous Illustrations. Third Edition. 5*s.*

XXX. **The Atomic Theory.** By Prof. Wurtz. Translated by G. Cleminshaw, F.C.S. Fourth Edition. 5*s.*

XXXI. **The Natural Conditions of Existence as they affect Animal Life.** By Karl Semper. With 2 Maps and 106 Woodcuts. Third Edition. 5*s.*

XXXII. **General Physiology of Muscles and Nerves.** By Prof. J. Rosenthal. Third Edition. With Illustrations. 5*s.*

D

XXXIII. **Sight:** an Exposition of the Principles of Monocular and Binocular Vision. By Joseph le Conte, LL.D. Second Edition. With 132 Illustrations. 5*s.*

XXXIV. **Illusions:** a Psychological Study. By James Sully. Second Edition. 5*s.*

XXXV. **Volcanoes: what they are and what they teach.** By Professor J. W. Judd, F.R.S. With 92 Illustrations on Wood. Third Edition. 5*s.*

XXXVI. **Suicide:** an Essay on Comparative Moral Statistics. By Prof. H. Morselli. Second Edition. With Diagrams. 5*s.*

XXXVII. **The Brain and its Functions.** By J. Luys. With Illustrations. Second Edition. 5*s.*

XXXVIII. **Myth and Science:** an Essay. By Tito Vignoli. Second Edition. 5*s.*

XXXIX. **The Sun.** By Professor Young. With Illustrations. Second Edition. 5*s.*

XL. **Ants, Bees, and Wasps:** a Record of Observations on the Habits of the Social Hymenoptera. By Sir John Lubbock, Bart., M.P. With 5 Chromo-lithographic Illustrations. Eighth Edition. 5*s.*

XLI. **Animal Intelligence.** By G. J. Romanes, LL.D., F.R.S. Third Edition. 5*s.*

XLII. **The Concepts and Theories of Modern Physics.** By J. B. Stallo. Third Edition. 5*s.*

XLIII. **Diseases of the Memory;** An Essay in the Positive Psychology. By Prof. Th. Ribot. Second Edition. 5*s.*

XLIV. **Man before Metals.** By N. Joly, with 148 Illustrations. Third Edition. 5*s.*

XLV. **The Science of Politics.** By Prof. Sheldon Amos. Third Edition. 5*s.*

XLVI. **Elementary Meteorology.** By Robert H. Scott. Third Edition. With Numerous Illustrations. 5*s.*

XLVII. **The Organs of Speech and their Application in the Formation of Articulate Sounds.** By Georg Hermann Von Meyer. With 47 Woodcuts. 5*s.*

XLVIII. **Fallacies.** A View of Logic from the Practical Side. By Alfred Sidgwick. 5*s.*

XLIX. **Origin of Cultivated Plants.** By Alphonse de Candolle. 5*s.*

L. **Jelly-Fish, Star-Fish, and Sea-Urchins.** Being a Research on Primitive Nervous Systems. By G. J. Romanes. With Illustrations. 5*s.*

LI. **The Common Sense of the Exact Sciences.** By the late William Kingdon Clifford. Second Edition. With 100 Figures. 5*s.*

LII. **Physical Expression: Its Modes and Principles.** By Francis Warner, M.D., F.R.C.P. With 50 Illustrations. 5*s.*

LIII. **Anthropoid Apes.** By Robert Hartmann. With 63 Illustrations. 5*s.*

LIV. **The Mammalia in their Relation to Primeval Times.** By Oscar Schmidt. With 51 Woodcuts. 5*s.*

LV. **Comparative Literature.** By H. Macaulay Posnett, LL.D. 5*s.*

LVI. **Earthquakes and other Earth Movements.** By Prof. John Milne. With 38 Figures. 5*s.*

LVII. **Microbes, Ferments, and Moulds.** By E. L. Trouessart. With 107 Illustrations. 5*s.*

MILITARY WORKS.

BRACKENBURY, Col. C. B., R.A. — **Military Handbooks for Regimental Officers.**

I. **Military Sketching and Reconnaissance.** By Col. F. J. Hutchison and Major H. G. MacGregor. Fourth Edition. With 15 Plates. Small crown 8vo, 4*s.*

II. **The Elements of Modern Tactics Practically applied to English Formations.** By Lieut.-Col. Wilkinson Shaw. Fifth Edition. With 25 Plates and Maps. Small crown 8vo, 9*s.*

III. **Field Artillery.** Its Equipment, Organization and Tactics. By Major Sisson C. Pratt, R.A. With 12 Plates. Second Edition. Small crown 8vo, 6*s.*

IV. **The Elements of Military Administration.** First Part: Permanent System of Administration. By Major J. W. Buxton. Small crown 8vo. 7*s.* 6*d.*

V. **Military Law:** Its Procedure and Practice. By Major Sisson C. Pratt, R.A. Second Edition. Small crown 8vo, 4*s.* 6*d.*

VI. **Cavalry in Modern War.** By Col. F. Chenevix Trench. Small crown 8vo, 6*s.*

VII. **Field Works.** Their Technical Construction and Tactical Application. By the Editor, Col. C. B. Brackenbury, R.A. Small crown 8vo.

BRENT, Brig.-Gen. J. L. — **Mobilizable Fortifications and their Controlling Influence in War.** Crown 8vo, 5*s.*

BROOKE, *Major, C. K.*—A System of Field Training. Small crown 8vo, cloth limp, 2s.

CLERY, *C., Lieut.-Col.*—Minor Tactics. With 26 Maps and Plans. Seventh Edition, Revised. Crown 8vo, 9s.

COLVILE, *Lieut.-Col. C. F.*—Military Tribunals. Sewed, 2s. 6d.

CRAUFURD, *Capt. H. J.*—Suggestions for the Military Training of a Company of Infantry. Crown 8vo, 1s. 6d.

HAMILTON, *Capt. Ian, A.D.C.*—The Fighting of the Future. 1s.

HARRISON, *Col. R.*—The Officer's Memorandum Book for Peace and War. Fourth Edition, Revised throughout. Oblong 32mo, red basil, with pencil, 3s. 6d.

Notes on Cavalry Tactics, Organisation, etc. By a Cavalry Officer. With Diagrams. Demy 8vo, 12s.

PARR, *Capt. H. Hallam, C.M.G.*—The Dress, Horses, and Equipment of Infantry and Staff Officers. Crown 8vo, 1s.

SCHAW, *Col. H.*—The Defence and Attack of Positions and Localities. Third Edition, Revised and Corrected. Crown 8vo, 3s. 6d.

STONE, *Capt. F. Gleadowe, R.A.*—Tactical Studies from the Franco-German War of 1870-71. With 22 Lithographic Sketches and Maps. Demy 8vo, 30s.

WILKINSON, *H. Spenser, Capt. 20th Lancashire R.V.*—Citizen Soldiers. Essays towards the Improvement of the Volunteer Force. Crown 8vo, 2s. 6d.

POETRY.

ADAM OF ST. VICTOR.—The Liturgical Poetry of Adam of St. Victor. From the text of GAUTIER. With Translations into English in the Original Metres, and Short Explanatory Notes, by DIGBY S. WRANGHAM, M.A. 3 vols. Crown 8vo, printed on hand-made paper, boards, 21s.

AUCHMUTY, *A. C.*—Poems of English Heroism : From Brunanburh to Lucknow ; from Athelstan to Albert. Small crown 8vo, 1s. 6d.

BARNES, *William.*—Poems of Rural Life, in the Dorset Dialect. New Edition, complete in one vol. Crown 8vo, 8s. 6d.

BAYNES, *Rev. Canon H. R.*—Home Songs for Quiet Hours. Fourth and Cheaper Edition. Fcap. 8vo, cloth, 2s. 6d.

BEVINGTON, *L. S.*—Key Notes. Small crown 8vo, 5s.

BLUNT, *Wilfrid Scawen.*—The Wind and the Whirlwind. Demy 8vo, 1s. 6d.

BLUNT, Wilfred Scawen—continued.

The Love Sonnets of Proteus. Fifth Edition, 18mo. Cloth extra, gilt top, 5s.

*BOWEN, H. C., M.A.—*Simple English Poems. English Literature for Junior Classes. In Four Parts. Parts I., II., and III., 6d. each, and Part IV., 1s. Complete, 3s.

*BRYANT, W. C.—*Poems. Cheap Edition, with Frontispiece. Small crown 8vo, 3s. 6d.

Calderon's Dramas : the Wonder-Working Magician — Life is a Dream—the Purgatory of St. Patrick. Translated by DENIS FLORENCE MACCARTHY. Post 8vo, 10s.

Camoens Lusiads. — Portuguese Text, with Translation by J. J. AUBERTIN. Second Edition. 2 vols. Crown 8vo, 12s.

*CAMPBELL, Lewis.—*Sophocles. The Seven Plays in English Verse. Crown 8vo, 7s. 6d.

*CERVANTES.—*Journey to Parnassus. Spanish Text, with Translation into English Tercets, Preface, and Illustrative Notes, by JAMES Y. GIBSON. Crown 8vo, 12s.

Numantia : a Tragedy. Translated from the Spanish, with Introduction and Notes, by JAMES Y. GIBSON. Crown 8vo, printed on hand-made paper, 5s.

CHAVANNES, Mary Charlotte. — **A Few Translations from Victor Hugo and other Poets.** Small crown 8vo, 2s. 6d.

*CHRISTIE, A. J.—*The End of Man. With 4 Autotype Illustrations. 4to, 10s. 6d.

Chronicles of Christopher Columbus. A Poem in 12 Cantos. By M. D. C. Crown 8vo, 7s. 6d.

*CLARKE, Mary Cowden.—*Honey from the Weed. Verses. Crown 8vo, 7s.

*COXHEAD, Ethel.—*Birds and Babies. Imp. 16mo. With 33 Illustrations. Gilt, 2s. 6d.

*DE BERANGER.—*A Selection from his Songs. In English Verse. By WILLIAM TOYNBEE. Small crown 8vo, 2s. 6d.

*DENNIS, J.—*English Sonnets. Collected and Arranged by. Small crown 8vo, 2s. 6d.

*DE VERE, Aubrey.—*Poetical Works.

    I. THE SEARCH AFTER PROSERPINE, etc. **6s.**
    II. THE LEGENDS OF ST. PATRICK, etc. **6s.**
    III. ALEXANDER THE GREAT, etc. **6s.**

The Foray of Queen Meave, and other Legends of Ireland's Heroic Age. Small crown 8vo, 5s.

Legends of the Saxon Saints. Small crown 8vo, 6s.

DOBSON, Austin.—**Old World Idylls** and other Verses. Sixth Edition. Elzevir 8vo, gilt top, 6*s.*

At the Sign of the Lyre. Fourth Edition. Elzevir 8vo, gilt top, 6*s.*

DOMETT, Alfred.—**Ranolf and Amohia.** A Dream of Two Lives. New Edition, Revised. 2 vols. Crown 8vo, 12*s.*

Dorothy : a Country Story in Elegiac Verse. With Preface. Demy 8vo, 5*s.*

DOWDEN, Edward, LL.D.—**Shakspere's Sonnets.** With Introduction and Notes. Large post 8vo, 7*s.* 6*d.*

Dulce Cor : being the Poems of Ford Bereton. With Two Illustrations. Crown 8vo, 6*s.*

DUTT, Toru.—**A Sheaf Gleaned in French Fields.** New Edition. Demy 8vo, 10*s.* 6*d.*

Ancient Ballads and Legends of Hindustan. With an Introductory Memoir by EDMUND GOSSE. Second Edition, 18mo. Cloth extra, gilt top, 5*s.*

EDWARDS, Miss Betham.—**Poems.** Small crown 8vo, 3*s.* 6*d.*

ELDRYTH, Maud.—**Margaret,** and other Poems. Small crown 8vo, 3*s.* 6*d.*

All Soul's Eve, "No God," and other Poems. Fcap. 8vo, 3*s.* 6*d.*

ELLIOTT, Ebenezer, The Corn Law Rhymer.—**Poems.** Edited by his son, the Rev. EDWIN ELLIOTT, of St. John's, Antigua. 2 vols. Crown 8vo, 18*s.*

English Verse. Edited by W. J. LINTON and R. H. STODDARD. 5 vols. Crown 8vo, cloth, 5*s.* each.

    I. CHAUCER TO BURNS.
    II. TRANSLATIONS.
    III. LYRICS OF THE NINETEENTH CENTURY.
    IV. DRAMATIC SCENES AND CHARACTERS.
    V. BALLADS AND ROMANCES.

ENIS.—**Gathered Leaves.** Small crown 8vo, 3*s.* 6*d.*

EVANS, Anne.—**Poems and Music.** With Memorial Preface by ANN THACKERAY RITCHIE. Large crown 8vo, 7*s.*

GOODCHILD, John A.—**Somnia Medici.** Two series. Small crown 8vo, 5*s.* each.

GOSSE, Edmund W.—**New Poems.** Crown 8vo, 7*s.* 6*d.*

Firdausi in Exile, and other Poems. Elzevir 8vo, gilt top, 6*s.*

GRINDROD, Charles.—**Plays from English History.** Crown 8vo, 7*s.* 6*d.*

The Stranger's Story, and his Poem, The Lament of Love : An Episode of the Malvern Hills. Small crown 8vo, 2*s.* 6*d.*

GURNEY, Rev. Alfred.—**The Vision of the Eucharist,** and other Poems. Crown 8vo, 5*s.*

A Christmas Faggot. Small crown 8vo, 5*s.*

HENRY, Daniel, Junr.—**Under a Fool's Cap.** Songs. Crown 8vo, cloth, bevelled boards, 5*s.*

HEYWOOD, J. C.—**Herodias, a Dramatic Poem.** New Edition, Revised. Small crown 8vo, 5*s.*

Antonius. A Dramatic Poem. New Edition, Revised. Small crown 8vo, 5*s.*

HICKEY, E. H.—**A Sculptor,** and other Poems. Small crown 8vo, 5*s.*

HOLE, W. G.—**Procris,** and other Poems. Fcap. 8vo, 3*s.* 6*d.*

KEATS, John.—**Poetical Works.** Edited by W. T. ARNOLD. Large crown 8vo, choicely printed on hand-made paper, with Portrait in *eau-forte.* Parchment or cloth, 12*s.* ; vellum, 15*s.*

KING, Mrs. Hamilton.—**The Disciples.** Eighth Edition, and Notes. Small crown 8vo, 5*s.*

A Book of Dreams. Crown 8vo, 3*s.* 6*d.*

KNOX, The Hon. Mrs. O. N.—**Four Pictures from a Life,** and other Poems. Small crown 8vo, 3*s.* 6*d.*

LANG, A.—**XXXII Ballades in Blue China.** Elzevir 8vo, 5*s.*

Rhymes à la Mode. With Frontispiece by E. A. Abbey. Elzevir 8vo, cloth extra, gilt top, 5*s.*

LAWSON, Right Hon. Mr. Justice.—**Hymni Usitati Latine Redditi** : with other Verses. Small 8vo, parchment, 5*s.*

Lessing's Nathan the Wise. Translated by EUSTACE K. CORBETT. Crown 8vo, 6*s.*

Life Thoughts. Small crown 8vo, 2*s.* 6*d.*

Living English Poets MDCCCLXXXII. With Frontispiece by Walter Crane. Second Edition. Large crown 8vo. Printed on hand-made paper. Parchment or cloth, 12*s.* ; vellum, 15*s.*

LOCKER, F.—**London Lyrics.** Tenth Edition. With Portrait, Elzevir 8vo. Cloth extra, gilt top, 5*s.*

Love in Idleness. A Volume of Poems. With an Etching by W. B. Scott. Small crown 8vo, 5*s.*

LUMSDEN, Lieut.-Col. H. W.—**Beowulf : an Old English Poem.** Translated into Modern Rhymes. Second and Revised Edition. Small crown 8vo, 5*s.*

LYSAGHT, Sidney Royse.—**A Modern Ideal.** A Dramatic Poem. Small crown 8vo, 5*s.*

MACGREGOR, Duncan.—**Clouds and Sunlight.** Poems. Small crown 8vo, 5*s.*

MAGNUSSON, *Eirikr, M.A., and* PALMER, *E. H., M.A.*—Johan Ludvig Runeberg's Lyrical Songs, Idylls, and Epigrams. Fcap. 8vo, 5s.

MAKCLOUD, *Even.*—Ballads of the Western Highlands and Islands of Scotland. Small crown 8vo, 3s. 6d.

MC'NAUGHTON, *J. H.*—Onnalinda. A Romance. Small crown 8vo, 7s. 6d.

MEREDITH, *Owen* [*The Earl of Lytton*].—Lucile. New Edition. With 32 Illustrations. 16mo, 3s. 6d. Cloth extra, gilt edges, 4s. 6d.

MORRIS, *Lewis.*—Poetical Works of. New and Cheaper Editions, with Portrait. Complete in 3 vols., 5s. each.
   Vol. I. contains "Songs of Two Worlds." Eleventh Edition.
   Vol. II. contains "The Epic of Hades." Twentieth Edition.
   Vol. III. contains "Gwen" and "The Ode of Life." Sixth Edition.

   The Epic of Hades. With 16 Autotype Illustrations, after the Drawings of the late George R. Chapman. 4to, cloth extra, gilt leaves, 21s.

   The Epic of Hades. Presentation Edition. 4to, cloth extra, gilt leaves, 10s. 6d.

   Songs Unsung. Fifth Edition. Fcap. 8vo, 5s.

   The Lewis Morris Birthday Book. Edited by S. S. COPEMAN, with Frontispiece after a Design by the late George R. Chapman. 32mo, cloth extra, gilt edges, 2s.; cloth limp, 1s. 6d.

MORSHEAD, *E. D. A.* — The House of Atreus. Being the Agamemnon, Libation-Bearers, and Furies of Æschylus. Translated into English Verse. Crown 8vo, 7s.

   — The Suppliant Maidens of Æschylus. Crown 8vo, 3s. 6d.

MOZLEY, *J. Rickards.*—The Romance of Dennell. A Poem in Five Cantos. Crown 8vo, 7s. 6d.

MULHOLLAND, *Rosa.*—Vagrant Verses. Small crown 8vo, 5s.

NOEL, *The Hon. Roden.* — A Little Child's Monument. Third Edition. Small crown 8vo, 3s. 6d.

   The House of Ravensburg. New Edition. Small crown 8vo, 6s.

   The Red Flag, and other Poems. New Edition. Small crown 8vo, 6s.

   Songs of the Heights and Deeps. Crown 8vo, 6s.

OBBARD, *Constance Mary.*—Burley Bells. Small crown 8vo, 3s. 6d.

O'HAGAN, *John.*—The Song of Roland. Translated into English Verse. New and Cheaper Edition. Crown 8vo, 5s.

PFEIFFER, *Emily.*—The Rhyme of the Lady of the Rock, and How it Grew. Second Edition. Small crown 8vo, 3s. 6d.

PFEIFFER, Emily—continued.

Gerard's Monument, and other Poems. Second Edition. Crown 8vo, 6s.

Under the Aspens: Lyrical and Dramatic. With Portrait. Crown 8vo, 6s.

*PIATT, J. J.—*Idyls and Lyrics of the Ohio Valley. Crown 8vo, 5s.

*PIATT, Sarah M. B.—*A Voyage to the Fortunate Isles, and other Poems. 1 vol. Small crown 8vo, gilt top, 5s.

In Primrose Time. A New Irish Garland. Small crown 8vo, 2s. 6d.

Rare Poems of the 16th and 17th Centuries. Edited W. J. LINTON. Crown 8vo, 5s.

*RHOADES, James.—*The Georgics of Virgil. Translated into English Verse. Small crown 8vo, 5s.

Poems. Small crown 8vo, 4s. 6d.

*ROBINSON, A. Mary F.—*A Handful of Honeysuckle. Fcap. 8vo, 3s. 6d.

The Crowned Hippolytus. Translated from Euripides. With New Poems. Small crown 8vo, 5s.

*ROUS, Lieut.-Col.—*Conradin. Small crown 8vo, 2s.

*SANDYS, R. H.—*Egeus, and other Poems. Small crown 8vo, 3s. 6d.

*SCHILLER, Friedrich.—*Wallenstein. A Drama. Done in English Verse, by J. A. W. HUNTER, M.A. Crown 8vo, 7s. 6d.

*SCOTT, E. J. L.—*The Eclogues of Virgil.—Translated into English Verse. Small crown 8vo, 3s. 6d.

*SCOTT, George F. E.—*Theodora and other Poems. Small crown 8vo, 3s. 6d.

*SEYMOUR, F. H. A.—*Rienzi. A Play in Five Acts. Small crown 8vo, 5s.

Shak 's Works. The Avon Edition, 12 vols., fcap. 8vo, cloth, 18s. ; and in box. 21s. ; bound in 6 vols., cloth, 15s.

*SHERBROOKE, Viscount.—*Poems of a Life. Second Edition. Small crown 8vo, 2s. 6d.

*SMITH, J. W. Gilbart.—*The Loves of Vandyck. A Tale of Genoa. Small crown 8vo, 2s. 6d.

The Log o' the "Norseman." Small crown 8vo, 5s.

Songs of Coming Day. Small crown 8vo, 3s. 6d.

Sophocles : The Seven Plays in English Verse. Translated by LEWIS CAMPBELL. Crown 8vo, 7s. 6d.

*SPICER, Henry.—*Haska : a Drama in Three Acts (as represented at the Theatre Royal, Drury Lane, March 10th, 1877). Third Edition. Crown 8vo, 3s. 6d.

Uriel Acosta, in Three Acts. From the German of Gatzkow. Small crown 8vo, 2s. 6d.

SYMONDS, *John Addington.*—Vagabunduli Libellus. Crown 8vo, 6*s*.

Tasso's Jerusalem Delivered. Translated by Sir JOHN KINGSTON JAMES, Bart. Two Volumes. Printed on hand-made paper, parchment, bevelled boards. Large crown 8vo, 21*s*.

TAYLOR, *Sir H.*—Works. Complete in Five Volumes. Crown 8vo, 30*s*.

Philip Van Artevelde. Fcap. 8vo, 3*s*. 6*d*.
The Virgin Widow, etc. Fcap. 8vo, 3*s*. 6*d*.
The Statesman. Fcap. 8vo, 3*s*. 6*d*.

TAYLOR, *Augustus.*—Poems. Fcap. 8vo, 5*s*.

TAYLOR, *Margaret Scott.*—"Boys Together," and other Poems. Small crown 8vo, 6*s*.

TODHUNTER, *Dr. J.*—Laurella, and other Poems. Crown 8vo, 6*s*. 6*d*.

Forest Songs. Small crown 8vo, 3*s*. 6*d*.
The True Tragedy of Rienzi : a Drama. 3*s*. 6*d*.
Alcestis : a Dramatic Poem. Extra fcap. 8vo, 5*s*.
Helena in Troas. Small crown 8vo, 2*s*. 6*d*.

TYLER, *M. C.*—Anne Boleyn. A Tragedy in Six Acts. Second Edition. Small crown 8vo, 2*s*. 6*d*.

TYNAN, *Katherine.*—Louise de la Valliere, and other Poems. Small crown 8vo, 3*s*. 6*d*.

WEBSTER, *Augusta.*—In a Day : a Drama. Small crown 8vo, 2*s*. 6*d*.

Disguises : a Drama. Small crown 8vo, 5*s*.

Wet Days. By a Farmer. Small crown 8vo, 6*s*.

WOOD, *Rev. F. H.*—Echoes of the Night, and other Poems. Small crown 8vo, 3*s*. 6*d*.

Wordsworth Birthday Book, The. Edited by ADELAIDE and VIOLET WORDSWORTH. 32mo, limp cloth, 1*s*. 6*d*. ; cloth extra, 2*s*.

YOUNGMAN, *Thomas George.*—Poems. Small crown 8vo, 5*s*.

YOUNGS, *Ella Sharpe.*—Paphus, and other Poems. Small crown 8vo, 3*s*. 6*d*.

A Heart's Life, Sarpedon, and other Poems. Small crown 8vo, 3*s*. 6*d*.

NOVELS AND TALES.

"All But :" a Chronicle of Laxenford Life. By PEN OLIVER, F.R.C.S. With 20 Illustrations. Second Edition. Crown 8vo, 6*s*.

BANKS, *Mrs. G. L.*—God's Providence House. New Edition. Crown 8vo, 3*s*. 6*d*.

CHICHELE, *Mary.*—Doing and Undoing. A Story. Crown 8vo, 4*s*. 6*d*.

Danish Parsonage. By an Angler. Crown 8vo, 6*s*.

HUNTER, Hay.—The Crime of Christmas Day. A Tale of the Latin Quarter. By the Author of "My Ducats and my Daughter." 1s.

HUNTER, Hay, and WHYTE, Walter.—My Ducats and My Daughter. New and Cheaper Edition. With Frontispiece. Crown 8vo, 6s.

Hurst and Hanger. A History in Two Parts. 3 vols. 31s. 6d.

INGELOW, Jean.—Off the Skelligs : a Novel. With Frontispiece. Second Edition. Crown 8vo, 6s.

JENKINS, Edward.—A Secret of Two Lives. Crown 8vo, 2s. 6d.

KIELLAND, Alexander L.—Garman and Worse. A Norwegian Novel. Authorized Translation, by W. W. Kettlewell. Crown 8vo, 6s.

MACDONALD, G.—Donal Grant. A Novel. Second Edition. With Frontispiece. Crown 8vo, 6s.

Castle Warlock. A Novel. Second Edition. With Frontispiece. Crown 8vo, 6s.

Malcolm. With Portrait of the Author engraved on Steel. Seventh Edition. Crown 8vo, 6s.

The Marquis of Lossie. Sixth Edition. With Frontispiece. Crown 8vo, 6s.

St. George and St. Michael. Fifth Edition. With Frontispiece. Crown 8vo, 6s.

What's Mine's Mine. Second Edition. With Frontispiece. Crown 8vo, 6s.

Annals of a Quiet Neighbourhood. Fifth Edition. With Frontispiece. Crown 8vo, 6s.

The Seaboard Parish : a Sequel to "Annals of a Quiet Neighbourhood." Fourth Edition. With Frontispiece. Crown 8vo, 6s.

Wilfred Cumbermede. An Autobiographical Story. Fourth Edition. With Frontispiece. Crown 8vo, 6s.

MALET, Lucas.—Colonel Enderby's Wife. A Novel. New and Cheaper Edition. With Frontispiece. Crown 8vo, 6s.

MULHOLLAND, Rosa.—Marcella Grace. An Irish Novel. Crown 8vo.

PALGRAVE, W. Gifford.—Hermann Agha : an Eastern Narrative. Third Edition. Crown 8vo, 6s.

SHAW, Flora L.—Castle Blair : a Story of Youthful Days. New and Cheaper Edition. Crown 8vo, 3s. 6d.

STRETTON, Hesba.—Through a Needle's Eye : a Story. New and Cheaper Edition, with Frontispiece. Crown 8vo, 6s.

TAYLOR, Col. Meadows, C.S.I., M.R.I.A.—Seeta : a Novel. With Frontispiece. Crown 8vo, 6s.

Tippoo Sultaun : a Tale of the Mysore War. With Frontispiece. Crown 8vo, 6s.

Ralph Darnell. With Frontispiece. Crown 8vo, 6s.

A Noble Queen. With Frontispiece. Crown 8vo, 6s.

The Confessions of a Thug. With Frontispiece. Crown 8vo, 6s.

Tara : a Mahratta Tale. With Frontispiece. Crown 8vo, 6s.

Within Sound of the Sea. With Frontispiece. Crown 8vo, 6s.

BOOKS FOR THE YOUNG.

Brave Men's Footsteps. A Book of Example and Anecdote for Young People. By the Editor of "Men who have Risen." With 4 Illustrations by C. Doyle. Eighth Edition. Crown 8vo, 3s. 6d.

COXHEAD, Ethel.—**Birds and Babies.** Imp. 16mo. With 33 Illustrations. Cloth gilt, 2s. 6d.

DAVIES, G. Christopher.—**Rambles and Adventures of our School Field Club.** With 4 Illustrations. New and Cheaper Edition. Crown 8vo, 3s. 6d.

EDMONDS, Herbert.—**Well Spent Lives :** a Series of Modern Biographies. New and Cheaper Edition. Crown 8vo, 3s. 6d.

EVANS, Mark.—**The Story of our Father's Love,** told to Children. Sixth and Cheaper Edition of Theology for Children. With 4 Illustrations. Fcap. 8vo, 1s. 6d.

JOHNSON, Virginia W.—**The Catskill Fairies.** Illustrated by Alfred Fredericks. 5s.

MACKENNA, S. J.—**Plucky Fellows.** A Book for Boys. With 6 Illustrations. Fifth Edition. Crown 8vo, 3s. 6d.

REANEY, Mrs. G. S.—**Waking and Working ;** or, From Girlhood to Womanhood. New and Cheaper Edition. With a Frontispiece. Crown 8vo, 3s. 6d.

> **Blessing and Blessed :** a Sketch of Girl Life. New and Cheaper Edition. Crown 8vo, 3s. 6d.

> **Rose Gurney's Discovery.** A Story for Girls. Dedicated to their Mothers. Crown 8vo, 3s. 6d.

> **English Girls :** Their Place and Power. With Preface by the Rev. R. W. Dale. Fourth Edition. Fcap. 8vo, 2s. 6d.

> **Just Anyone,** and other Stories. Three Illustrations. Royal 16mo, 1s. 6d.

> **Sunbeam Willie,** and other Stories. Three Illustrations. Royal 16mo, 1s. 6d.

> **Sunshine Jenny,** and other Stories. Three Illustrations. Royal 16mo, 1s. 6d.

STOCKTON, Frank R.—**A Jolly Fellowship.** With 20 Illustrations. Crown 8vo, 5s.

STORR, Francis, and TURNER, Hawes.—**Canterbury Chimes ;** or, Chaucer Tales re-told to Children. With 6 Illustrations from the Ellesmere Manuscript. Third Edition. Fcap. 8vo, 3s. 6d.

STRETTON, Hesba.—**David Lloyd's Last Will.** With 4 Illustrations. New Edition. Royal 16mo, 2s. 6d.

WHITAKER, Florence.—**Christy's Inheritance.** A London Story. Illustrated. Royal 16mo, 1s. 6d.

PRINTED BY WILLIAM CLOWES AND SONS, LIMITED, LONDON AND BECCLES.

www.ingramcontent.com/pod-product-compliance
Lightning Source LLC
Chambersburg PA
CBHW020117030726
47498CB00006B/2155